Broken Heart

Broken Heart

Reed Family Series, Book 1

Tyora Moody

Tymm Publishing LLC
Columbia, SC

Broken Heart
Reed Family Series, Book 1

Copyright © 2016 by Tyora Moody

Broken Heart is a work of fiction. Names, characters, places and incidents either are products of the author's imagination or are used fictitiously. Any resemblance to actual persons, living or dead, events, or locales is entirely coincidental.

Published by Tymm Publishing LLC
701 Gervais Street, Suite 150-185
Columbia, SC 29201
www.tymmpublishing.com

Cover Design: TywebbinCreations.com
Content Editing: Robin J. Caldwell
Copy Editing/Proofreading: Felicia Murrell

The Lord is close to the brokenhearted
and saves those who are crushed in spirit.
— *Psalm 34:18 NIV*

Chapter 1

Wednesday, August 19 at 8:15 a.m.

"Go ahead! Answer your phone. You and I both know what's really important to you."

No, he didn't just say that. Detective Jo Reed-Powell barely heard her ringing cell phone as she clenched her fists. She shouted, "Don't you dare make this about my work! You slept with another woman." Jo reached for the ceramic bowl on the counter and heaved it towards her husband.

Bryan Powell leapt to the side as the bowl smashed into the doorframe, sending leftover pancake mix and small ceramic pieces flying across the floor. Her husband stared back at her. His emotions warred on his face. Without a word, he grabbed his keys and walked out of the kitchen towards the garage.

Tears streamed down the side of her face as she heard Bryan's Ford Mustang roar to life. The rage swirling inside her was so overwhelming. Jo closed her eyes and leaned against the kitchen counter for support. She gasped for breath as waves of anger threatened to buckle her knees. Finally, she let out a wounded cry that rose from deep inside and wept. *How could you do this to us?*

In all seven years of their marriage, Jo had never been suspicious of Bryan's behavior before. She'd never had a reason to be concerned. But in recent months, he'd become distant. This morning, he had left his phone on the kitchen counter. When Jo heard the tiny bell tone, she picked up his phone to bring it to him, but for some reason felt compelled to look at the text message.

I have no regrets. A.

She knew the text was from Bryan's co-worker, Alexis Davenport. The text could have been innocent, but it didn't take any of Jo's detective skills to recognize the guilt on Bryan's face when she asked him about the message. Bryan probably would have never confessed the affair if she hadn't interrogated him about his whereabouts yesterday. It was so unlike Bryan to forget to pick up their son from Jo's parents' house. Everyone including B.J.

was upset and worried. This week had already been a struggle with the new school year starting for the first-grader.

Besides that was *her thing* to lose track of time.

Jo lost count of the number of times she was so focused on a case she completely forgot about time. Yesterday, her steadfast husband forgot about his own child because he was entangled with another woman.

Bryan tried to convince Jo that he was ending the affair.

He should have never started the affair.

Her cell phone rang again. She lifted her head from the counter, not sure if she should answer it or not. Jo pulled her phone from the clip on her pants and looked at the screen. It was her partner, Pete McConnelly, no doubt calling about a brand new crime scene. Jo closed her eyes, praying for her voice to sound normal. She answered the phone on the third ring. "What you got, Pete?"

"Everything all right, kid? Usually, you would have answered by now."

She cleared her throat, trying to shake the emotions clinging to her. "Sorry, Pete. Rough morning. Where do you need me?"

"Pine Woods Park Apartments. You're not going to like this one, Jo."

"I'll be there soon." Jo frowned after Pete hung up. She clipped the phone back to her side, thinking about Pete's statement. There weren't many crimes that surprised her anymore. Bryan's affair did surprise her and Jo wasn't sure how she was going to be able to cope the rest of the day.

She cringed at the broken bowl on the floor thinking matters could have been worse. She'd made it a habit to leave her gun at work since she didn't like keeping the weapon around her son. She'd been with the Charlotte-Mecklenburg Police Department for nine years and knew how quickly domestic violence could elevate. Maybe Bryan's leaving was wise.

Jo went over to the sink and splashed her face with cold water. She patted her face dry with a paper towel. One thing for sure, she couldn't leave the mess since it was her turn to pick up B.J. from her parents' house today. Jo was thankful the school bus had already picked up her son before she discovered the incriminating text message on Bryan's phone.

She grabbed the broom and swept up the broken pieces. Then she wet paper towels and wiped up all the pancake mix she could see on the wall and floor. Satisfied with her quick clean up, Jo grabbed her keys and headed out to her own car in the garage. As she stepped outside to lock the side door, the late summer humidity crept through her cotton shirt. Jo's physical discomfort was no match for the growing unease inside her mind. After she climbed into the Ford Taurus, she searched for Pine Woods Park Apartments and pulled up the route on the GPS. She said a silent prayer before starting the engine. She had no choice but to put on her detective hat now. She would deal with her cheating husband later.

Wednesday, August 19 at 9:43 a.m.

Jo's mind wandered as she drove down I-77. Bryan had introduced Alexis Davenport to her at last year's company Christmas party. Jo immediately pegged the curvy woman as trouble. It was the nature of Jo's job to profile everyone she came across. A few months ago she'd even told Bryan how uncomfortable she was with him going to a conference in Atlanta with Alexis. Jo was pretty secure, but it just didn't feel right for Bryan to be traveling with an attractive woman.

At the time, Bryan had the nerve to bring up

her partner. To Jo, there was no comparison. Her partner, though a ladies' man, was fifteen years older and more like a father-figure. Jo certainly was not hanging out after work or going on out-of-town trips with her partner. Their relationship was strictly professional.

She checked her mirrors and merged into the right lane so she wouldn't miss the exit. It was almost ten o'clock when Jo pulled into the parking lot already occupied by several other law enforcement vehicles. Her body still felt shaky from her emotional outburst earlier. She inhaled deeply and then exhaled to calm her nerves before stepping out of the car. Jo had a reputation for being tough, despite her petite size. Respect was important to her.

She flashed her badge at the officer and then crossed under the yellow tape. The crime scene wasn't too far from the city, tucked away in a woodsy area behind the Pine Woods Park Apartments. Jo saw her partner break away from talking to an officer and walk towards her. Pete was a tall, good looking man with gray temples. He liked to joke if he ever lost weight, he could probably pass for George Clooney. He certainly didn't have a problem catching women. Currently, he was working on his girlfriend becoming wife number three. He studied her. "Are you all right? Allergies?"

Jo appreciated Pete's concern. As senior detective, he'd been very supportive of her career's ups and downs, but right now she decided it was best to ignore her partner's question. She wasn't really sure how she was feeling and wished her issues were only allergy-related. Jo pulled on latex gloves, fitting them to her hands and responded, "What's so special about this one?"

Pete looked at her as though he was deciding what to say. "You'll see."

Jo followed Pete, thinking she didn't need any more surprises today. The shade from the large pine trees projected more gloom than usual over the crime scene. Jo noted CSI had marked off what appeared to be distinct footprints in the soft dirt that no grass covered. Jo stopped and looked behind her to the parking lot. She observed the layout of the apartment windows and then turned her attention to where the body rested down a hill. The wooded area was pretty hidden, but Jo hoped someone saw or heard something.

As Jo drew closer to the crime scene, her eyes focused on the blond-haired woman who appeared to be lying on the ground on top of a rug. The victim was dressed in a hot pink dress that was pushed up to the top of her legs. One foot was bare, while the other foot was clad in a black high heel pump with hot pink soles. Jo thought something was oddly familiar about the woman. Sadly, she'd seen too many of these crime scenes.

The medical examiner, Lou Reynolds, was taking notes as a criminal scene investigator placed each of the woman's hands in paper bags.

Jo asked, "Lou, does it look like she was sexually assaulted?"

Lou peered over his glasses and responded. "I'll know more when I get her back to the examining room."

Jo examined the rug, which was beige with burgundy and black patterns. "Well, this is definitely not the crime scene since someone wrapped her in this rug and dumped her here."

Pete stared down at the victim. "Real pretty girl. We're trying to see if she lived in one of these apartments."

Jo heard Lou say, "You have to see this, Jo."

Jo's senses went on high alert. She glanced over at Pete's grim face and then at Lou who looked equally as serious. Jo moved up closer to the woman's head. She leaned over and stared down at the woman's face, which was smeared with mascara as if she'd been crying. Jo thought she must have been really scared. The left side of the woman's face was bruised as if someone had hit her. Smeared blood was visible under her nose towards her top lip. She wondered if the woman had been on a date with someone she knew who later assaulted her.

Jo's eyes traveled down. She almost gasped when she saw the ligatures around the victim's neck. The distinctive roped pattern was fresh. Jo had seen similar markings before on three other victims last year. They were also blond and all similar in age to this current victim.

Jo stood up straight. Beads of sweat broke out on her forehead. She was aware of Lou and Pete watching her, but she could only focus on the image in her mind of the person responsible for those deaths. Thanks to her and Pete, that man was sitting in a jail cell awaiting trial. Jo was the one who read him his rights as they made the arrest nine months ago on what had become the biggest case of her career. The media had drawn attention to the strangulations for months. A copycat killer was not what Jo needed right now. A brief thought fluttered into her mind. Or was this a copycat?

No! Jo refused to believe she'd missed any details of the case that took over her life last year.

Chapter 2

Wednesday, August 19 at 3:35 p.m.

Jo tried to focus on the elderly woman in front of her. Lit only by a floor lamp in the far corner and a small television, the living room was cozy and tidy. Apparently, if Mrs. Bostick's Pomeranian hadn't decided to run towards the trees this morning, the victim would not have been found until much later. The dog barked insistently from a bedroom at the back of the apartment. Jo was really hoping Mrs. Bostick was one of those neighbors who liked to peek at her neighbors through blinds. The blinds on the window that faced the crime scene area outside were closed shut.

"Snooki just kept barking and barking. It was so early in the morning and I didn't want to disturb anyone. So I had to go get her since she wouldn't come when I called." The woman held her crossed arms close to her body. "I thought it was odd seeing a rug out there. When I got closer, then..." The woman's voice trailed off. "I saw the arm."

Jo felt bad that Mrs. Bostick had found a dead body near her apartment. She asked, "Mrs. Bostick, are you sure you didn't notice any strange cars or individuals last night?"

"No. I'm sorry. I'm usually up late some nights, but I went to bed early last night. Did that poor woman live around here? This is a big place so I don't know everyone."

"We're not sure yet. We'll be doing our rounds." Jo stood and pulled out her business card. "Mrs. Bostick, thank you for your help. If you think of anything, please don't hesitate to call me."

"I hope you find out who did this. I feel bad for her family."

Jo nodded and let herself out of Mrs. Bostick's apartment. She met up with Pete on the other side of the apartment complex.

Pete said, "Let's head over to see if Lou has found anything. I talked to the apartment manager. He'll get us a listing of the residents. I hate when we get a case like this. It may be too hopeful to think someone killed her in one of these apartments and decided to dump her in the back."

Jo nodded. Her mind had wandered back to this morning's events. She focused on Pete's face and commented, "People have done stranger things. Somebody had to see something."

They arrived separately at the Mecklenburg County Medical Examiner's Office. As she caught up with him, Jo noticed Pete eyeing her as though he expected her to explode. Her mother always told her she was never good at hiding her emotions. Jo let out a long sigh as they approached the medical examiner's area.

"You all right, kid?"

Jo grimaced. Pete and she had been partners for five years. After a very tense first year, Jo had proven herself worthy of respect from her senior detective partner, but he still insisted on calling her kid. Really, Pete referred to everyone who was a decade younger than him that way. Jo had become accustomed to it, along with Pete's other idiosyncrasies.

"Yeah, I'm fine. Let's see what Lou has for us."

Pete opened the door. Jo crossed her arms as if to protect herself and entered. It still wasn't easy seeing a body covered by a white sheet under the stark light as they listened to the medical examiner's report. Being from a large close family, it never failed to hit Jo that the person lying on the table was someone's child, spouse, sibling or friend. It was her job to find the person responsible for so much pain and suffering.

Jo examined their vic's face, wondering who the woman had encountered last night. The victim's skin had taken on a grayish-blue hue, but Jo could tell the young woman had been pretty. There was more bruising around the left side of the victim's face that Jo didn't catch before. *Why did this person choose to strangle this woman? What was his motive?*

Last year, Jo investigated and helped arrest Jeffrey Maddock who now sat behind bars awaiting trial. Maddock was the tall, dark and handsome type. He appeared warm and friendly to most, but was really a cold and calculating person. The former real estate agent had a pattern of reacting violently to rejection. He snuffed out three victims by strangulation. Jo was convinced there were more than three, possibly in other states since she discovered Maddock had also lived in Georgia, Texas and Virginia.

The evidence they gave the prosecution was solid. The women were killed in their own homes by someone they obviously knew and willingly let inside. Jo was able to make a connection to someone all the women had in common in their lives. Maddock's good looks and charms made it easy for him to entrap the single, career-oriented women. She discovered he liked blondes, especially those who had a striking resemblance to Maddock's abusive, deceased mother. Witnesses confirmed Maddock had romantic contact with all three victims. That's where he made his mistake.

So, who was this?

Jo turned her attention to Lou, who had just walked in. "Lou, do you have anything for us?"

"You guys need to give me time on my report. We just sent our findings to the crime lab for further analysis."

Pete asked, "You can at least tell us if she has been sexually assaulted."

Lou shook his head. "No DNA evidence found."

Jo's stomach did a somersault. *This is going to be a difficult case.*

Pete interrupted her thoughts and asked Lou the exact questions swirling in her mind. "What are you thinking? I think we were all surprised on the similarities of this crime scene to Maddock's victims."

Lou looked at Pete. "The victim is young and blond, and yes cause of death is strangulation. But, no need to jump to conclusions."

Pete raised his eyebrow. "The perp is about to go to trial in a month. We don't want to give any ammunition for reasonable doubt to his defense team."

Jo shook her head. "No chance for doubt. Maddock was connected to all three of those women. Lou, you helped gather the forensic evidence. There are very clear differences with this vic, right?"

Lou looked over his glasses at Jo and Pete. "On the surface, it looks and feels the same. But, there are some differences." Lou picked up the victim's hands, "She has fibers under her fingernails. I would say she clawed at the same rug she was wrapped in probably trying to get away."

"See this?" Lou pointed to some scratches around the side of the ligature on the victim's neck. "She was trying to claw at whatever was around her neck. It could be a rope similar to what Maddock used. Really, the rope can be purchased at a hardware store or Walmart. Pretty common." Lou stared at the victim for a moment. "I wouldn't be surprised if she scratched her killer. We will need to wait on the DNA results from the crime lab though."

Jo shook her head. "You're right. Maddock's victims didn't have any signs of this much struggle because he tied their arms behind them. Maddock also put something in their drink to subdue them."

Pete spoke up. "How long has she been dead, Lou?"

Lou crossed his arms and looked at both of them. "When we found her, rigor mortis had set in, that takes two to six hours. It was warm last night so that sped up the process. I would say anywhere between midnight and the early hours this morning is when she died. This woman was alive yesterday."

Lou lifted the sheet. "Look at the left side of her face with the bruising and the rigor mortis on this side of her body. Someone hit her on the left here, and connected with her nose. Probably with his fist. She must have been on her left side for some time, possibly during the transport of her body. You can see where the blood settled on her left."

Jo responded, "We need to find the original crime scene. Thanks, Lou."

Lou nodded. "I'm depending on you two to

identify this woman so we can notify next-of-kin. We want someone to lay her to rest."

As they left, Pete had a few choice words. "I had some doubts for a minute there. Still, I haven't seen a strangulation like that since Maddock's last victim. I don't want to think copycat, but that detail was released to the media."

Jo didn't believe in coincidences. "I admit it's crazy that the victim fits Maddock's m.o., but this is too different. Maddock has been in prison for nine months. I doubt this is a copycat."

Pete threw up his hands. "You never know, kid. Remember Maddock is a psychopath. He often manipulated people to get what he wanted. I'm sure he isn't a fan of that jail cell and is trying to figure out how to become a free man."

As they walked out the building, Jo's thoughts about her husband returned. She needed to go pick up B.J. from her parents' home.

Before they reached their cars, Pete asked, "Are you okay? You seem distracted today."

Jo wasn't sure it was best to confide in her partner. Married and divorced twice, Pete had an affair while married to his first wife, interestingly enough with his first female partner. The tables were turned on him with the second wife who had an affair with a doctor. Pete still hadn't recovered since two of his children were being raised by the man. No, she didn't need Pete giving her any of his bitter advice.

"Just an argument with Bryan."

"Must have been serious. You never let anything distract you. I hope you guys make up. We need to stay on top of this case or we're going to feel some pain if the press gets hold of any similarities to Maddock's victims."

Her cell phone buzzed a distinct ringtone, but she ignored it. "There isn't anything to worry about. Although with her being a Jane Doe, we will need help identifying her. Look, I need to pick up B.J. I'm sorry it's been an off day."

"We're human, kid. Tell B.J. Uncle Pete says hello. I'm going to check back around the apartment complex and the crime scene before calling it day. People should be arriving home, so I can ask around more. See you at the office tomorrow."

After Jo climbed into her car, she looked down at the phone. She already knew by the special ringtone she'd missed Bryan's call. At least he left a message. She pressed the voicemail button and placed the phone to her ear. Tears sprang to her eyes as she heard his voice. He sounded like the same person, but somehow he'd become someone she didn't recognize anymore.

"Jo, I'm sorry. I'm really sorry. I've been back to the house to pick up a few things. I'm staying away for a few days. I think it's the best thing to do. I know you probably hate me right now. Tell B.J. I love him."

Sorry! He was sorry. How was she going to explain to B.J. where his daddy had gone? What would she tell her parents?

Jo wasn't finished with her questions. She had to know why Bryan started the affair in the first place and what prompted him to end it yesterday.

Her mind struggled with a memory. She had confessed to Bryan her astonishment at how fast their six-year-old son had grown. With her thirty-fifth birthday approaching, it was like her biological clock had been ticking louder and louder. She loved B.J., but she longed for a girl. Jo told Bryan she was ready to have another child.

At the time, Bryan's quietness puzzled her. It was as if he doubted her desire to have another child. It was true Jo had been hesitant for years, wanting just to enjoy B.J. But she never wanted him to remain an only child. She leaned on the steering wheel and moaned, "You were having an affair then, Bryan."

Chapter 3

Wednesday, August 19 at 6:00 p.m.

Jo pulled her car into her parents' driveway. She turned the engine off and looked up at the brick home where she and her three siblings had grown up. Jo had always felt overshadowed by her ambitious older sister, Asia. Later when the twins, Cori and Toni, came along, Jo grew into being the withdrawn middle child. It took her some time to convince herself that she could enter the police academy after stumbling around for many years.

Jo stepped out of the car and walked around the side of the house. She heard her son's sweet laughter. She paused on the back patio and watched her dad attempt to play catch with B.J. Her son wasn't too successful at catching the ball. Jo was happy to see her dad, Justice Reed, up and about lately. Many days her dad still seemed depressed about his early retirement as police chief. He retired under a firestorm of accusations. Two white cops were accused of unlawful force against a young African American man in their custody resulting in his death. Even though the mayor had quietly urged Jo's dad to retire, it didn't stop the public's growing disdain of the police.

"B.J. is good for him." A voice behind Jo said.

Jo turned. Her mom had stepped out onto the patio. "B.J. loves his grandpa and it doesn't hurt that he is the first and only grandchild. We need to get my other siblings married so they can give you guys a slew of grandkids."

Jo's mother asked, "Are you okay, Jo?" Vanessa Reed knew all of her children too well. Jo and her siblings all agreed it was very difficult to keep anything from their mother. Vanessa placed her hand on Jo's shoulders. "Why don't we go inside and sit for a minute. Let B.J. have some more time with his grandpa."

Jo followed her mother from the patio into the kitchen, instantly feeling like she was fourteen instead of thirty-four years old. The smells coming from the kitchen felt like home. "Who are the sweet potato pies for? You usually don't like to bake in the summer."

Her mother grinned. "It was a special request. Tomorrow night we're having the Pastor Appreciation Dinner for Pastor Freeman."

"That's right." Jo had missed attending Victory Gospel Church last Sunday and was looking forward to going this coming Sunday with Bryan and B.J.

Bryan has left our home. Oh yeah...and had an affair.

Her mother asked, "Was Bryan okay yesterday? He had us all concerned."

Not able to keep her emotions in check in front of her mother, Jo shook her head as she blinked back tears.

"Jo, what's going on?"

Jo took a deep breath. "I guess I might as well let you know. Bryan left. At least for a few days he said."

Her mother's eyes grew wide with questions. "Left?"

Jo blew out a breath, trying to hold back the tidal wave erupting inside of her. "It took me pulling my bad cop role, but Bryan admitted that he was busy with his co-worker, which is why he forgot about his own son." Jo added in barely a whisper, "Busy, so he says, ending an affair."

Jo's mother placed her hand on her head as if to stop a raging headache. "Oh my, Jo. How could he?"

Jo plopped down in a chair at the kitchen table. "Yeah, I have been asking myself that all day. You know, we found a young woman today whose family may not know she's dead. I'm trying to do my job and..."

Her mother pulled out the other chair and sat. She didn't say anything, just took Jo's hand.

It dawned on Jo that her mother knew exactly what this felt like. As much as she loved her dad, Jo still didn't like the years of pain he brought her mother with his affair. To this day, she still didn't understand why her mother stayed. The most difficult part of her dad's affair for her mom was the son born from his mistress. While her mother had learned to accept Jackson, it had been an awkward journey. Jo's older sister, Asia, still didn't fully accept their half-brother, but Jo and the twins over the years had grown fond of their older half-brother who they called Jax.

As she thought of her half-brother, Jo wondered if Bryan had even used protection. She didn't know if she had her mother's forgiving heart if B.J. had a new brother or sister in the works from another woman. Jo noticed she had a pounding discomfort in her temples. "Do you have anything for a headache? I'm worn out from thinking too much."

Her mother walked towards a cabinet and grabbed a bottle of Tylenol. After handing Jo the pills and a glass of water, she sat and asked, "Jo, what are you going to do?"

Jo shook out two pills from the bottle, swallowed them and gulped down the water. "I don't know. Even if the affair is supposedly over now, Bryan replaced me with another woman. A woman who obviously had no regrets about being with a married man. This morning Bryan had the nerve to make me feel like my job was more important to me. I know I pulled some long hours and I get too caught up in cases. He knew that when he married me. He also knows he and B.J., you, dad, my brothers and sisters... Family is everything to me."

Her mother shook her head. "That wasn't fair of him. I don't know what he was thinking, but I do want you to pray about what to do next."

Jo stared at her mother. "You stayed with dad. I know it must have been really hard finding out he had another child with someone else before I was born. Even though I was only three years old when I first met him, I remember wondering where Jax came from and why he didn't live with us. Jax is only a year older than me and his mother was difficult. Did you stay because of Asia and me?"

Her mother looked at her. "Mostly. I wanted to give up, many times more than you know. I kept praying about what to do. I felt God leading me to stay and to work it out. His ways are higher than ours, Jo. Despite praying, I still was not truly able to forgive Jax's mother until her breast cancer diagnosis last year. It was like God was preparing me to be there for Jax when she died."

Vanessa looked away and swallowed. "Besides, if I had left your father, we would have never have had the twins. Your sister and brother were born after your father and I renewed our vows. The years before were so painful, but I believe all my children are destined for good things." Her mother rubbed her shoulder. "Give it time. Pray. And, don't move too rashly."

"Mommy." B.J. burst forward with Jo's dad in tow.

Jo reached out her arms as her son ran towards

her for a hug. "Are you ready to head home, kiddo? Go grab your backpack."

"Okay." B.J. ran into the family room.

Her dad stood by the counter. "I hope one of these sweet potato pies are staying here because I sure could use a slice."

Her mother grabbed a towel from the table and swiped it at Jo's father. "Don't you think about touching anything on that counter, Justice Reed."

Her dad shook his head. "This woman won't let me have anything."

B.J. ran back in. "Mommy, Grandpa is going to have burgers and hot dogs this weekend. Can we come?"

Jo looked at her mom and her dad. Usually all of her siblings would come for the barbecue feast. Jo wouldn't mind catching up with them, but now she wasn't sure she wanted the whole clan to know about Bryan yet.

Her dad asked, "Jo, can you come? You're not working this weekend are you? I told you not to let the job take over." Her dad peered at her a little closer. "What's going on?"

The new case loomed in Jo's mind. "I may need to work. We got a brand new case today with a Jane Doe."

Her dad frowned. "A Jane Doe? Those take time, Jo. What does Bryan say about it?"

Jo snapped, "I doubt he cares." She looked away from her dad to face B.J. Looking like Bryan's mini-me, her son's eyes were inquisitive.

"Let's go, B.J. We can pick up a pizza on the way home."

B.J. jumped in the air and squealed, "Pizza!" He took off towards the door.

Jo hugged her mom, "Thanks for the talk."

She turned to her dad and hugged him. "Thanks for looking out for B.J. Mom can fill you in, but things may be different for a while."

Her dad nodded. "Not a problem. You know we're here for you. Still be careful, don't burn yourself out."

"I will, but I have a feeling I need to stay on top of this new case."

She also needed this case to keep her going. Her heart may be broken, but she was determined to find justice for the Jane Doe they found today. She didn't want to fail at doing her job at least.

Chapter 4

Thursday, August 20 at 9:30 p.m.

Bryan had been gone for over twenty-four hours. He never called on Wednesday night leaving her with a very perplexed B.J., full of questions she couldn't answer. She was grateful her mother offered to pick up B.J. and keep him until the weekend.

After questioning more people at the apartment complex on Thursday, Jo almost welcomed the silence at home especially since she still had no new leads on the case. Despite her circumstances and Bryan's absence, Jo convinced herself to enjoy the rarity of being home by herself. She called and talked to B.J. and her mother. Afterwards, she took a long hot bath and settled into bed.

The brief window of peace disappeared when Jo

recognized the ringtone on her phone. She started to ignore Bryan's call, but then wanted to hear what he had to say.

"Hello, Jo. May I speak to B.J.?" Bryan asked.

Bryan might as well have punched her in the stomach. *So that's how this is going to go?* She swallowed before answering. "B.J. is staying with my parents. You can call and talk to him, if my mother lets you. You know they go to bed early."

"I guess that means you were working tonight."

A surge of hurt and anger struck Jo. "What exactly are you trying to say? You were the one having an affair. Wait, oh I forgot, ending an affair and you forgot to pick up your son. You left our home and didn't bother to call your son last night, who by the way wanted to know where his daddy was."

"I was just making a comment, Jo. I know I've messed up."

"But you want to blame me. I can hear it in your voice. You will not mess with me about my parenting skills too."

Bryan responded with silence on the other end.

"You know what, I can't with you. I just can't. If you were so unhappy with me, you could have been honest. What happened to our promise to always talk to each other? You didn't have to have sex with another woman." Jo ended the call, gripping the phone in her hand. She wasn't sure she wanted Bryan to come back. *Where is he anyway? Did he really break up with Alexis or did he change his mind?*

Jo curled into the fetal position and cried into her pillow. She was not a woman who cried easily. Growing up, she was the tomboy and athlete. And to her parents chagrin, she was the rebellious one. Somehow she found purpose following her dad's footsteps in law enforcement. Always the late bloomer, she found her first love later than most, and that one true love was Bryan.

God, I don't know what to do? I still love him, but I feel like my marriage is over.

Friday, August 21 at 10:30 a.m.

For the second night in a row, Jo barely slept. With great effort, she pulled herself out of bed. She hadn't worked out at the gym in two days. To add more insult to her weary body, on the way to work she purchased two jelly donuts from Dunkin Donuts along with black coffee. Jo couldn't remember the last time she'd eaten donuts.

When she arrived at work she ignored Pete's

wide eyes. Without fail, Pete had a Hardee's steak and egg biscuit on his desk. A true southerner, Pete believed in a hearty breakfast, and usually ridiculed Jo about her fruit and granola bars.

"No quinoa and flax seed this morning, kid?"

Jo glared at him and bit into the jelly donut. She savored the sweet jelly, licking her fingers. She'd sat at her desk all morning reviewing her notes. The property manager at the apartment complex didn't recognize the victim, but he said people came and went as their leases expired so it was hard to keep track. The victim could have been carried either from an apartment or transferred by a car. Either way, it would have taken some effort to get the body, wrapped in a rug, down into the woodsy area.

She didn't know why, but Jo couldn't help but compare the crime scene to Maddock's victims. All of the women were found in their homes. It was obvious each of the women knew their killer because there were no signs of forced entry. Very different crime scenes. She was feeling less anxious than she had been yesterday about this case affecting Maddock's trial.

Jo pushed her chair away from the desk and lifted her arms above her head to stretch. It was time for more coffee. Her morning sugar rush had faded. She wasn't trying to drink the sludge already sitting in the coffee pot so she started a fresh brew.

"Now that's what I'm talking about. Fresh coffee. You're a saint, Jo."

Jo turned around to laugh. "I wish. I wasn't trying to drink that mess people around here call coffee."

Detective Darnell Jackson placed his mug on the counter. "You're smart, too!"

Jo couldn't help but feel a little bit of Darnell's joy. "You are still acting like a newlywed. How long has it been?"

Darnell grinned, "Seems longer, but Candace and I have been married almost two years."

Jo smiled. "I'm happy for you both. It's good to keep that glow."

"Oh I plan too. This is a second marriage for both of us. Candace and I want it to be the last one. You know? Until death do us part thing. Hey, you know I'm glad I ran into you today. We're starting the basketball teams up at Victory Gospel. You think Bryan wants to join us again this year?"

Jo felt her jaw twitch as she struggled to keep smiling. "He might. I'll ask him about it." Jo turned to pick up the pot. "Coffee's ready."

Darnell held up his mug as Jo poured. "Thanks, Jo. I hear Maddock is finally going to get his day in court soon."

Happy Darnell changed the subject, Jo poured coffee into her cup. "Yep. We provided solid evidence, so the D.A. should be able to convince the jury to do the right thing. Besides, I don't think the defense has much of a case."

Darnell sipped his coffee. "Maddock didn't confess, but anyone can tell he's guilty. You and Pete did a good job getting that guy. He's a real piece of work. Thanks again for the fresh coffee. Please don't forget to ask Bryan about coaching. We could use his help."

Jo nodded, feeling a knot form in her stomach as Darnell walked away. *Does Bryan have any idea what he's done?* If their marriage fell apart, there would be rippling effects. Victory Gospel was the Reeds' family home church.

On her way back to her desk with her refilled coffee mug, she saw Pete walking towards her holding something in his hand.

"We may have an I.D. for our girl."

Jo sat her coffee mug down on her desk. "Really? How? Who is she?"

Pete held out his hands. "Whoa, slow down. You

are going to want to take this in nice an easy." He passed a photo to Jo. "First, here she is."

Jo grasped the photo. She immediately recognized the young woman to be their victim. Not only did she have a beauty queen smile, but the woman had been a participant in some type of pageant. She was wearing a tiara and had a bright pink sequined dash across her pale pink gown. Her blue eyes sparkled.

This woman was certainly Maddock's type, Jo thought. "What's her name?"

Pete cleared his throat before he responded. "Laura. Laura Finney."

Jo stared at Pete. "Finney? She wouldn't be related to...?"

Pete crossed his arms and nodded. "Senator Morris Finney."

"You have got to be kidding me?" Jo felt nauseous. She probably shouldn't have eaten those two jelly donuts.

"I wish I was. Her mother called to say their daughter was missing this morning. Police chief put Captain on red alert. The captain was the one who came to me with that photo. The parents will be heading to the morgue soon to confirm."

Jo rubbed her forehead. "I'm glad we may know

who she is now. We can start narrowing down her schedule and talk to people who knew about her plans on Tuesday night. Remember Senator Finney is not a fan of this department. I should know. That guy worked with the mayor to force my dad to retire. He'll make this investigation more difficult."

"I know. I talked to the captain. He agreed we need to keep a lid on some of the details and move at lightning speed as soon as we have confirmation. Come on. Let's head over to the morgue, so we can talk to the Finneys."

Jo and Pete arrived in time to watch the Finneys walk in with Lou. Based on the wail that ripped from Mrs. Finney a few minutes later, it appeared their victim was Laura Finney. They waited for a few minutes before approaching the grieving parents. Senator Finney was a man who enjoyed public service and liked the spotlight. Right now as he held his wife, Jo recognized grief and a smoldering anger behind the man's blue eyes.

Pete led the conversation, "Senator and Mrs. Finney, we're sorry about your loss. I'm Detective McConnelly and this is Detective Reed-Powell. We hoped to ask you a few questions."

Jo jumped right into the first question, "Any idea

who Laura could have been with on Tuesday evening?"

Mrs. Finney lifted her tear-stained face. Probably in her late forties or early fifties, she was still a beauty herself. "She said she was going out with friends. She was supposed to head back to Duke this weekend and wanted to spend time with her high school friends. They are all going into their senior year of college."

Jo hadn't realized the victim was that young. She made a mental note that Maddock's victims were in their late twenties and were established career women. She asked, "Can you give us names?"

Senator Finney frowned, not looking at Jo, he stated, "None of my daughter's friends would harm her."

Puzzled, Jo looked at Pete before responding to the senator. "Her friends may know someone Laura was seeing that you didn't know."

Mrs. Finney yelped, "Laura's engaged. Her fiancé adores her."

Senator Finney gripped his wife's arm. "Where did you find her?"

Jo noticed the senator addressed his questions mainly to Pete as though he didn't want to acknowledge her. She wondered if he recognized her name, Reed. Jo did look like her father.

Pete cleared his throat. "We can't share too many details, Senator. However, the evidence, so far, points to the crime scene being different from where she was found. Any help you can give to help us to pinpoint her whereabouts on Tuesday evening would be appreciated."

Jo added, "We want to find the person responsible as soon as possible."

The family was grieving and maybe they needed time to process their daughter's death. But something didn't feel right to Jo. Her parents were already on the defensive, which meant there was a lot more to find out about former beauty queen and college student, Laura Finney.

Chapter 5

Saturday, August 22 at 9:30 a.m.

Jo stopped by her parents' Saturday morning to spend time with B.J. Her parents were having a barbecue, but Jo planned to work for a few hours. They needed to make some progress on the case since they had only identified Laura Finney yesterday. B.J. was still wearing his Spider-Man pajamas and finishing up a bowl of Cheerios. "Mommy, where's Daddy and when can I come home?"

"I'm picking you up this afternoon. Didn't Daddy call you?"

B.J. nodded. "I talked to Daddy last night. He said he was away on business, but he didn't say when he would be back."

Jo had doubts about the business part. "I'm sure Daddy will be back soon, honey."

Her mother walked up to the kitchen table and picked up the breakfast dishes. "B.J., Uncle Cori will be here soon. I just talked to him. Your Aunt Asia and Aunt Toni will be here later too."

"Yay!" B.J. asked, "What about Uncle Jax?"

Jo looked at her mother. It had been awhile since she'd seen her half-brother.

Jo's mother placed the dishes in the sink and turned around. "I believe Grandpa called Jackson, but I'm not sure if he will drive up from Atlanta or not. Now B.J., go see if Grandpa needs help."

"Okay!"

After B.J. ran from the kitchen, her mother looked at Jo. "You're not going to work too long today, are you? You have been pulling a lot of hours this week."

"I'll be back in time for the feast. So Bryan called?"

Her mother nodded. "Bryan called here last night to talk to B.J. I did mention the barbecue today. Your dad does it every summer around this time especially since you and Bryan have been doing the 4th of July the past two years. It just came out. I can tell he felt awkward. Have you two talked?"

"He had an affair and left the house. Kind of hard to just talk."

"Well, you both need to talk at some point even if you need a third party. Marriage counseling can be arranged at the church. The longer you don't deal with the root issues, the harder it will be to save the marriage. That's if you want to save it."

Her mother looked at her with concern. "I know how you feel, Jo. Believe me. I also know how you will let your anger override reasoning. I don't want you to do anything you'd regret. These situations can wreck a person mentally. Have you been praying?"

"I'm trying. I get angry and then end up feeling guilty as if I did something wrong."

"You're not the blame for Bryan's choices."

"I know that, but last year was a difficult time. I hoped it would get better after we arrested Maddock. I've been guilty of forgetting to pick up B.J. a few times myself."

Vanessa glared at Jo. "Please consider what I said. You do need to work on what to do next. Just wallowing in anger and guilt is what's going to eat you both alive, Jo. It's not going to help B.J., who's going to end up being in the middle of two very bitter people."

Jo looked at the time on her phone. "I know, I know. Look I have to go. Pete and I need to touch base with the Finneys. We were urged to give them space yesterday, but we have lost so much time already on this case."

Her mother grimaced. "I don't like the man, but I'm sorry about his daughter. The captain couldn't assign this to someone else?"

"Mama, it was already my case. I'm going to see this through. It's what I do."

"I know. I do hope you find who did this to their daughter."

"Me too."

As Jo drove out to the Finneys' home she couldn't help but think about how much she didn't like the senator. No one in the Reed family had much love for Senator Finney. With a blanket statement, he had ended Justice Reed's career as police.

He has no control and has let officers disgrace our city and state.

Even after her father fired the cops involved in the shooting death of the young man, Senator Finney used the incident to secure his third term in office by calling for her dad's resignation and making way for a clean sweep of change in the Charlotte-Mecklenburg Police Department. Her dad retired a month before the election.

Still, Jo would treat this case as any of her other cases. She wanted justice served even for the senator.

Saturday, August 22 at 11:07 a.m.

Jo and Pete approached the front door together. A Hispanic woman who appeared to be in her thirties answered the door. She led them to a sitting area, where Mrs. Finney sat alone. Dressed only in a large white robe, Mrs. Finney held a china teacup in her lap as she stared out of a bay window that faced a garden outdoors. Mrs. Finney turned to look at them as they approached. Her eyes looked vacant.

"Mrs. Finney, thank you for letting us view Laura's room," Jo said. "Did you think of anything else about Tuesday? Anything unusual?"

Mrs. Finney shook her head as if to shake away her thoughts. With a deep sigh she leaned forward and placed her teacup on the table. "Laura was excited to go out with her friends. I remember she couldn't decide on what outfit to wear. She left a mess in her closet as usual."

Jo thought about how Laura left the house. "Did Laura drive her car?"

Mrs. Finney shook her head. "No, one of the girls picked her up. Her car is outside."

Pete asked, "You mind if I check out her car?"

Jo added, "I would like to see Laura's room." Mrs. Finney led Jo up the stairs to Laura's bedroom. When Mrs. Finney opened the door, Jo could tell it was a room that had grown with Laura. As she stepped inside, she could almost imagine when the walls were probably painted some pastel color with stuffed animals on the bed. The room she stood in now was still girly, but more sophisticated for a young woman. Fuchsia and brown squares covered the back of the queen-size bed, while two walls were painted a solid fuchsia and one wall a solid brown.

It was bold and funky. Jo would have chosen similar colors if she had a girl. At twenty-one years old, Laura may have outgrown her teenage posters, because there were none on the wall. There were a variety of photos of Laura, some of her as cheerleader, at a dance recital and when she was a little girl. All types of trophies and tiaras lined one wall on shelves.

Mrs. Finney spoke from the doorway. "It's just how she left it."

Jo was so engrossed in studying the room, she forgot the woman was behind her. "Laura accomplished a lot. Do you mind if I look around alone? I'll try not to disturb much."

Mrs. Finney turned slowly as if she didn't want to leave. She grabbed the door handle and closed the door behind her.

Jo sighed deeply. She didn't like looking through someone's personal space after they died, but it was a way to find clues. They didn't have many leads on what happened until they could talk to Laura's friends and her fiancé. Jo decided to start with what would have the most information about Laura. She sat at the desk and flipped open the pink paisley covered laptop. There was no login on the screen after the laptop booted.

The wallpaper showed Laura with a young man. Jo observed the blond young man. The striking couple resembled a real-life Ken and Barbie. She clicked on Laura's email and scrolled through her inbox. There was nothing that struck Jo as unusual from the subject lines. She snapped the laptop closed and decided to take the laptop to a tech to examine the email. She wanted to take a better look at the bedroom.

Jo slid open a door that revealed a walk-in closet. Indeed, Laura had a difficult time choosing what to wear. Several dresses lay on an ottoman in the middle of the closet. All types of shoes lined one wall. One pair of shoes caught Jo's eyes because they were on the floor next to the ottoman. The sling back sandals had an even higher heel than the one heel Laura was found wearing.

She walked out of the closet over to the vanity table. Makeup and costume jewelry lay out in the open. It was probably just Jo, because she was more of a plain Jane, but it felt to her like Laura had gone through a lot of trouble to get dressed up on Tuesday evening. Did Laura's friends also go through this much trouble? Jo looked forward to meeting them.

Something sparkled from one of the drawers of an open wooden jewelry box. Jo frowned as she pulled the drawer out. She reached inside and lifted out a one carat diamond ring. *Is this Laura's engagement ring?*

Laura was supposedly out with friends but where was her fiancé? It seemed strange to Jo that

Laura would leave home without her engagement ring. An engagement ring was meant to flaunt, especially one like this. She wondered how Laura's fiancé would have reacted if he saw Laura without the ring on her finger.

Chapter 6

Saturday, August 22 at 5:35 p.m.

"Alright, kid. I'm going to enjoy what weekend I have left. You should do the same." Pete placed his Carolina Panthers hat on his head. "My lady isn't too happy with me."

Jo looked at her phone, checking the time. Her family probably had already started the festivities. She looked at Pete. "This job isn't easy on relationships."

Pete grinned. "I should know. Wife number one and two still remind me. My three kids don't have much to say to me most of the year unless they're short on cash, of course."

Jo tilted her head in sympathy. "But you've met the right woman this time, right?"

"I'll find out soon enough. All I can do is try. I

don't like being alone. You need to be getting along too. No need to keep Bryan waiting."

Jo bit her lip. She hadn't shared her predicament at home yet. "Enjoy the rest of your weekend, Pete."

After Pete left, Jo turned her attention back to the evidence board. There were too many loose ends and not many leads. She looked at the photos of footprints that were around the body. Since it had rained softly on Monday, the shaded ground around Laura's body was still soft. She hoped CSI would be able to share a lead about the type of shoe that made the footprint. Jo thought the thread looked like a sneaker.

She really wanted to know where the rug came from that Laura was wrapped in, and why were the woods behind the Pine Woods Park Apartments selected as the dumping ground. Though Laura's phone had probably been destroyed, Jo put in a request for the phone records so they could triangulate her whereabouts, and possibly the actual murder scene. They still had several interviews to conduct. Hopefully then they would have a better timeline.

Jo shook her head. It was time to call it a day. Plus, she was ready to eat her dad's grilled masterpieces. She grabbed her bag and headed towards her car. Jo sped down I-77 to her parents' home. Her parents and siblings liked Bryan, at least when he hadn't given them a reason not to.

Early in their marriage, Bryan tried and failed at managing his own web design company. Clients would often fail to pay on time or not at all, resulting in a lot of debt and past due bills. Jo wanted Bryan to do what he loved and stood by him despite her family's concern. No one was more grateful than she when he found a position as a web developer at Progressive Media.

Bryan worked there for three years. He seemed to love it, especially since Progressive Media was a hip place that offered flexible hours. All was fine until Alexis was hired as a project manager almost a year ago.

I'll be glad to be with my family. I'm tired and worn out thinking about Bryan and his affair with Alexis.

She pulled into her parents' driveway, climbed out of her car and went around the back. Her nose was drawn towards the charcoal grill smoke. Her dad wore his red apron wrapped around his waist. He was chatting with some of his retired buddies. She waved to the group of men she'd known since childhood, and headed inside the house.

B.J. was playing a video game with his Uncle Cori. Jo stopped and grinned as she watched her son and younger brother duke it out. Cori was twenty-six years old, unmarried and the smartest person she knew. No one in the family was surprised when he decided to go into forensics. He was always a science fiction geek.

"Don't hurt him too bad, B.J."

B.J. laughed, "I won two games."

"Ah, sis. What kind of kid do you have here? He's too smart for six years old."

Jo patted her brother on the head. "Sounds like he gets some of that from his Uncle Cori. I remember you being just like this at six years old." Jo was also sure her competitive younger brother was letting B.J. win.

Cori turned and grinned, "Hey, I'm a good influence."

"I don't know. B.J. is starting to follow your Star Wars obsession."

"That's not bad, sis." Cori's face turned serious. "Hey!" He observed B.J. before turning around. "Are you okay? I can't believe you-know-who."

Jo guessed her mother filled in Toni and Cori on the news of Bryan's affair. Jo was almost eight years older than the twins, but it often felt like her mother had a closer relationship with her precocious younger siblings. Jo's heart melted over her brother's concern. "Me neither. I'm as good as I can be. Thanks for asking."

Jo headed into the kitchen. Toni jumped up from where she sat with a plate of food. Jo's younger sister was by far the free spirit in the family. Her thick natural hair was placed high above her head in a large puff. Toni used her artistic skills successfully as a valuable forensic artist for CMPD. Their dad often proudly declared how all of his children were crime fighters with their various roles in law enforcement.

Toni bent down to hug Jo. For some reason, all of her siblings had their dad's height while Jo inherited their mother's short stature. "Jo, you finally made it. Girl, Mama was going to have me go drag you out of that building."

Their mother grinned. "Your sister is exaggerating. I hope your day was productive."

Jo grabbed a ginger ale from the fridge and popped the lid. She answered her mother, "Sort of. There are still a lot of unanswered questions." Jo drank from the can enjoying the sharp taste of the bubbles. She glanced at the row of grilled chicken, hamburgers, and hotdogs on the counter. She was really hungry.

As Jo reached for a plate, she heard her older sister bellowing from the other room. "I'm here. I hope you people didn't eat *all* the food." Asia stepped into the doorway of the kitchen looking like a fashion model. Dressed in khaki pants and a red short-sleeved shirt, Asia had her matching khaki jacket folded over her arms. She placed the jacket and her large brown bag on a kitchen chair.

Jo eyed her sister who worked as an assistant D.A. at the district attorney's office. "You're just getting here too? Don't tell me you were working on a Saturday too?"

Asia kicked off her three-inch high pumps before sitting. "Girl, you know the district attorney's office is getting ready for Jeffrey Maddock's trial in a few weeks. You of all people should be happy. By the way, you did a great job gathering the evidence for the case. My boss is ecstatic about getting this trial going."

Jo added some potato chips next to her hamburger. "Well thanks, sis. You actually sound proud of me."

Asia grabbed a plate. "I am proud of you. It was you who picked up on the romantic connections between Maddock and those women. I tell you every time I see that man, he makes my skin crawl. It's sad because he is good looking, but he's so evil."

Their mother spoke from the table. "That's the way evil is packaged. Often looks good on the outside."

Jo sat and dived into her food. As she chewed, she thought about Bryan's attraction to his colleague Alexis. She was a beautiful woman, but that was no excuse for Bryan straying away.

Toni nudged her. "How are you, Jo? Mama told us about Bryan."

Asia swung around from the counter, "What about Bryan? I haven't heard anything." She stared at Jo.

Jo attempted to swallow the food in her mouth, but a lump had suddenly formed in her throat making it difficult to swallow. The vibe of the kitchen was warm and cozy with the camaraderie of her sisters and her mother, now the atmosphere seemed to suffocate her.

Toni answered for her. "Bryan cheated with that woman we saw at the 4th of July barbecue."

Asia put her hand on her hips. "That heifer! Jo, I told you something was up with her."

Jo cringed, not sure if she wanted to laugh or cry.

Asia was right. Alexis had seemed glued to Bryan's side that day. Bryan had told her they were talking about work.

Their mother looked at her oldest daughter. "Asia, that was not necessary."

Asia took a seat with her plate. "Mama, come on. You know you probably called her the same thing. Mama tries to be sanctified about what she says. You know I could have called her something else."

Their mother shook her head. "Asia, just enjoy your meal. Jo's had a hard time as it is."

Asia wasn't one to ever be quiet, which was why she was the lawyer in the family. She chewed thoughtfully on her grilled chicken sandwich. "Jo, what are you going to do? I have plenty of divorce lawyers I can recommend."

Jo glared at her older sister. "I honestly haven't had time to process what to do. I'm kind of still in shock."

Their mother stood and started clearing the table. "Jo, that's why I asked you to pray and look into marriage counseling."

Asia smirked. "Counseling? Mama, you think they can work this out just like..."

Their mother's glare towards Asia left all three sisters quiet.

Finally, she responded, "Like your father and me. Every marriage doesn't have to crumble into a divorce. Sometimes these situations are a wakeup call to let God come in and be the center where He was not allowed to be present before."

Jo looked at her mother. Guilt shrouded her conscience. She hadn't wanted to admit it, but Bryan and she had been slowly gliding apart for some time. She had not prayed for her marriage the way she had in the beginning. B.J. was born and then her cases kept coming. Bryan's work could be time-consuming on occasion. Life snuck in and without her realizing it, an opening was left for the enemy to walk right through to steal, kill and destroy her marriage.

Suddenly, Jo felt like curling up in her own bed. She picked up her plate and tossed it in the garbage. "It's been a long day. I think B.J. and I need to head home."

Her mother walked over and hugged her. "Please get some rest. Maybe we will see you both in church tomorrow."

Jo hugged her back. "I'll try."

She exchanged hugs with both of her sisters. The men were a little difficult about the hugs, but Jo's mother and sisters insisted on hugs even if they had just argued with each other. Her mother helped her gather B.J.'s things and buckled him into the backseat of the car. B.J. slept soundly as Jo drove home. She was grateful since she didn't know if she could handle any of her son's questions about his daddy.

She desperately needed eight hours of sleep. For a change, Jo didn't want to think about the Finneys or the upcoming Maddock trial or Bryan. As she turned into her driveway, she pressed the garage opener, and was startled to see Bryan's Mustang. She thought he would have stayed away longer.

B.J. stirred in the backseat as Jo pulled into the garage. In a sleepy voice he said, "Mommy, look! Daddy's home."

Jo shut off the engine and looked over at Bryan's car. She wondered what this meant and if she had to deal with the inevitable tonight.

Chapter 7

Monday, August 24 at 6:45 a.m.

Smells of bacon wafted into Jo's nose as she struggled to wake up. She lazed in bed feeling more normal than she had in a week. When she turned to the side of the bed where Bryan slept, her false sense of normalcy faded. He'd slept in the guest bedroom since he came back Saturday night. After staring at his pillow for a few sad seconds, she sat up and rubbed her eyes. She reflected on their awkward weekend as a family.

Even though he was back, there wasn't much said between them on Saturday night and all of Sunday. They spent the weekend avoiding each other. Both evenings Bryan tucked B.J. into bed, while she turned in for the night. Both nights, she'd listened to B.J.'s laughter and Bryan's deep voice telling him a story.

Despite a lack of sleep Saturday night, Jo woke up determined to attend Sunday services at Victory Gospel, mainly because she wanted to get out of the house away from Bryan. So yesterday morning without bothering Bryan, Jo had quietly dressed B.J. and herself and left a note. Even though many people at church asked about him, Jo realized there was no way she could have sat next to Bryan. She kept looking back wondering if he was going to show up. She sat with her family and listened intently to Pastor Jonathan Freeman as he preached about David, a man after God's own heart. David had made mistakes that cost him, but God remained faithful to His promises.

Jo couldn't help but wonder if she'd made some mistakes that had cost her. She knew in her heart her role as a detective was her calling. It's what she loved. If she was really honest, Bryan had been slowly growing resentful of her career. And last year during the investigation that led to Maddock's arrest, Jo sensed a shift in their relationship. She couldn't shake the idea that she had a role in neglecting her own marriage.

Jo groaned. *I have to get up and go to work. I can't keep doing this to myself. He cheated, not me.*

She pushed the covers away and slid to the floor on her knees. She prayed for strength and for the ability to face Bryan. After showering, Jo headed into the kitchen where Bryan was helping B.J. get his backpack on his back.

"Mommy, Daddy said I don't need to take the bus to Grandpa and Grandma. He's going to pick me up."

Jo looked at Bryan, "Are you leaving the office early today?"

He didn't look directly at her. "I'm working from home this week."

Was this his way of avoiding Alexis? "You have not done that in a while. You sure that's okay?"

"I cleared it with Benny."

"Daddy, I hear the bus. I have to go now."

"Okay. Tell your mom goodbye."

B.J. ran over to Jo. "Bye, Mommy. See you later."

Jo hugged her son. "Have a good day, baby."

Bryan said, "Can you call your mom and let her know they don't need to watch B.J. this week?"

"Okay." There was a time when Bryan was comfortable talking to her parents himself, but he probably knew she'd shared his infidelity with her family.

She watched as her son and husband went outside to the bus. She looked at the almost finished pancakes on B.J's plate. Bryan was a good cook. He often cooked breakfast on the weekend, never a weekday. She knew Bryan intensely loved their son and like she did sometimes, probably cooked their son's favorite breakfast to make-up for not being around.

She prayed that B.J. was unaware of any tension between his parents.

Jo grabbed a coffee cup from the cabinet and poured coffee. As she sipped the bitter warm liquid, she looked around the kitchen wondering how long Bryan had been up. Did he have trouble sleeping too?

He should.

Bryan entered the kitchen, but paused in the doorway as if he was nervous to come near her. It was less than a week ago when she sent that ceramic bowl of pancake mix towards his head. Jo's anger still lingered, but she was not planning to lose control again. "I'm not going to throw anything else at you, Bryan."

He stared at her and then tilted his head down.

Bryan cleared his throat. "I don't blame you if you do."

Jo sat her cup on the counter. "Where were you?"

Bryan's lifted his head. "What?"

"You were gone for three nights. Where were you?" Jo gripped the mug feeling the warmth stinging her fingers and palms. "Were you with Alexis? Still trying to decide who you want?"

Bryan's eyes grew wide. "I stayed at a hotel. Alone. I told you it's over. She was never anything to me."

"She doesn't mean anything to you, but she has no regrets sleeping with a married man."

"Well, I do have regrets. I made a mistake one time and for the past few months I have tried to separate myself from Alexis, which is hard to do when you work with someone," Bryan sighed. "I went to try to reason with her last Tuesday. I had already asked Benny to take me off a project with her, but she still...kept indicating she was interested."

Jo frowned. "So you're telling me you slept with her one time and that was that? Is that supposed to make me feel any better? It sounds like she has developed feelings for you. I hope she isn't crazy too."

Bryan shook his head. "No, of course not. It's been awkward at work. I told her we needed to go back to being professionals. I was married and I shouldn't have fallen into temptation. Time just slipped by. I would have never forgotten B.J. doing something like *that*."

"But you did have sex with her? How long ago was this *one time*?"

Bryan crossed his arm as if to protect himself. "It was during the conference in Atlanta."

Jo stepped away from the counter towards Bryan. She thought back to earlier in the summer. "That was the last week in June. You came home in time enough to get ready for the 4th of July party."

"It's no excuse, but we had been drinking."

Jo yelled and flailed her arms up in the air. "You don't drink!"

"Not in a while, no, I haven't. I don't know why I decided to drink."

"So I should just forgive you and forget about this because you were drinking? You know it occurred to me that you have been distant since then. I didn't know why."

Jo walked towards her husband. "I know the

Maddock case was a lot and that I was not here. Do you remember what I mentioned to you once he was arrested? In fact, the conversation came up again a month ago right after B.J.'s birthday."

Bryan looked away. "You said you wanted us to get our family time back. That you thought it was time B.J. had a sister or brother."

Jo choked. "Isn't that what you want?"

Bryan's face crumbled. "Yes. I want you and B.J. in my life. I made a mistake and I tried to fix it."

Jo pointed her finger. "You tried to hide it too. I don't care if it was one time and you were drinking. Bryan, my trust has been broken. I even told you when I met Alexis that something about her made me uncomfortable. I wasn't jealous. I was telling you from my gut instinct."

Bryan took a moment before responding. His voice was low, barely above a whisper. "So what do you want me to do, Jo? I can't change what I did."

Jo stared at him.

He couldn't expect her to just accept his explanation that he'd been drinking. That was just plain pathetic. He wasn't accepting full responsibility for his actions and the fact that she'd warned him how she felt about Alexis.

"I don't know. I just know we will never be the same again." Jo walked out the kitchen. As she walked down the hallway, she wiped the tears blurring her vision. Once inside *their* bedroom she headed towards the bathroom. She closed the door and slid down to the floor, sitting on the fluffy blue rug beneath her. She needed to get ready for work, but she wanted to curl into a ball. She lifted her face towards the ceiling.

God, how can I ever trust him again?

Chapter 8

Monday, August 24 at 1:18 pm

The Finneys had the memorial service for Laura at their home. Jo sat next to Pete in the back of the room observing the immediate family and their guests. Jo's heart felt so heavy, she could have been mourning herself. There was a war going on inside her with one side trying to convince her that her marriage was dead. Jo pushed away the thoughts clawing at her to focus on the people who had attended Laura's memorial service.

After the service, the guests had gathered in a great room in the middle of the Finneys' home. A portrait of Laura sat on an easel by the entrance. Laura's makeup and skin were flawless as her long blond hair hung across her shoulders. For some reason, Laura's eyes appeared more seductive than the youthful look in the beauty pageant photo they had on the evidence board. Once again, Jo had the impression there were two sides to Laura. *Most people have two sides.* Jo hoped Laura's secret side would reveal more about what happened to her.

Jo searched the room and found Mrs. Finney in one of the sitting areas surrounded by three young women. Jo noticed Senator Finney was not nearby, which was probably a good thing. She looked back at Pete who was filling up a plate of food. She gestured to him to meet her over near Mrs. Finney. After zigzagging around the crowded room, Jo approached with Pete trailing behind.

Mrs. Finney stood. Her makeup was meticulously done, her blond hair swept up into a ponytail. Laura had been a younger version of her mother. "Detectives, thank you for coming. Please meet Laura's friends."

The woman appeared a bit too chipper for a grieving mother. Jo glanced at the glasses sitting on the table and wondered if Mrs. Finney had taken another substance with her glass of wine.

Jo tuned in as Mrs. Finney introduced the young women. Sarah Anderson was a blond. She looked so similar to Laura she could have been her sister. Micah Jacobs appeared to be a mixed African

American woman with long dark curly hair that partially covered her light caramel face.

Mrs. Finney turned to the third woman and seemed to hesitate. "And this is Clarice Rivers."

"Reece," The young woman snapped. "I go by Reece now, not Clarice."

Mrs. Finney placed her hands on her chest as if she was offended. She turned from *Reece* and tried to smile, but appeared to want to cry.

All three girls looked somber and as if they had been crying. Something about Reece made Jo think the young woman was uncomfortable being at the memorial, as if she felt out of place. Reece's green eyes darted back and forth behind royal blue frames. She was the shortest of the three young women and her short, black pixie haircut made her appear more tough than cute. She was dressed in all black, but Jo sensed wearing black was her normal fashion statement the majority of the time instead of just memorial service clothing.

Despite Reece's demeanor, the person Jo was really looking for didn't seem to be present in the room. Jo asked Mrs. Finney, "Where is Laura's fiancé, Matthew Vaynor?"

Mrs. Finney blinked. "Matt couldn't stay. He's very distraught, as you can imagine."

Jo looked over at Pete. He raised his right eyebrow. The fiancé was high on their list to talk to since there was more than likely a male involved in Laura's death. It was common to interview the significant other like a spouse or a boyfriend.

"No worries. We'll reach out to Matt later." Jo looked around the room and turned to Mrs. Finney, "Is there a room where we can talk one-on-one with the girls?"

Mrs. Finney seemed flustered, "Do you really have to do this now?"

Pete spoke up, "We just have a few questions about Laura. I'm sure these girls want to help."

Reece asked, "Do I need a lawyer?"

Strange question. This girl was definitely going to be interesting to interview. Jo forced a smile, "We simply want to find out what happened to Laura. Isn't that what we all want?" By the head nods, Jo assumed everyone agreed. "Good. Sarah, we'll start with you."

Once situated in what appeared to be Mrs. Finney's office, Pete agreed to let Jo take the lead with questions since the girls would be more comfortable talking with her. He sat in a chair behind the desk so he could observe and munch on the food he'd just collected.

Jo looked at Sarah who stood in the corner as if she didn't want to be there. "Come take a seat across from me, Sarah."

Sarah wiped her eyes and sat quickly on the couch.

Jo sat on the chair perpendicular to the couch. She pulled out her recorder and her notebook. "Do you mind if I record our conversation?"

Sarah shook her head.

"Thank you." Jo pushed the record button. "How long have you known Laura?"

"We've known each other since we were six years old. People always thought we were sisters."

Jo commented, "I can see the resemblance. You probably knew her well. When was the last time you talked?"

Sarah bit her lip. "In person? Probably Monday afternoon. We went to the gym together."

"Weren't you all together on Tuesday evening? I thought that's why Mrs. Finney asked you to be here," Jo asked.

It took a few seconds before Sarah answered. "We had plans for Tuesday night, but Laura cancelled. She didn't say, but I assumed she wanted to meet with someone else."

Jo glanced at Pete. He cocked an eyebrow. Jo

looks back at Sarah. "A man? Someone besides her fiancé?"

Sarah nodded. "She definitely wasn't planning to meet with Matt. She would have said so. I knew when she was vague or secretive that usually meant it wasn't any of my business."

Laura was cheating on her fiancé. That would explain the engagement ring left behind. Jo wondered why Laura accepted the engagement if she wasn't ready to commit. "Sarah, have you ever seen her with another man?"

Sarah nodded. "Not on a date, but we were running one morning a few weeks ago and a guy came up behind us. He scared me to death, but I could tell Laura knew him and was thrilled to see him. I walked behind while they walked and talked together. I couldn't blame her for liking him. He was good-looking."

"Can you describe him?"

"I remember he was tall, taller than Matt. Matt's six feet one, I think. This guy had dark hair and he had blue eyes. Really blue eyes."

Jo froze. She thought about Jeffrey Maddock. Sarah could have been describing his features. *That isn't possible because Maddock is in prison.* Jo didn't look back at Pete, but she wondered what he was thinking. This case wasn't anything like Maddock's victims, so Jo wasn't sure why she kept having these moments.

Sarah blew out a breath like she'd been running. "I thought the guy had to be wearing contact lens to be honest. Just something about his eye color looked off to me. I could tell he was more mature than Matt. Matt is my cousin, but he can be a jerk. Anyway, after the guy left, Laura was all smiles."

"She never mentioned his name?"

Sarah frowned. "No. She said she had met him earlier in the summer when we went to this new club. It's the place where Reece works. I don't remember seeing him then, but I wasn't in the best condition that night. Too much to drink. I'm not sure how I even got home that night."

Jo noted that Laura and Sarah were two friends who liked to have a good time. "Just to confirm you only talked to her Monday afternoon? When did she officially cancel the plans for Tuesday night?"

"She texted a message early Tuesday afternoon. I didn't really want to go out on a Tuesday night anyway. I just started this new job and wanted to wait until the weekend."

"Makes sense. Thanks, Sarah. That will be all for now. Will you be going back to school soon?"

Sarah looked at Jo. "I dropped out of UNC last year."

"Oh, I'm sorry to hear that."

Sarah shrugged. "No big deal. Laura was the smart one. At least most of the time." Sarah bit her lip as tears rolled down her face. "I still can't believe she's gone."

Jo nodded, "I'm sorry for your loss, Sarah." She watched Sarah as she left the room wondering how close she really was to Laura. There seemed to be some animosity.

Ten minutes later, Jo questioned Micah. "How long have you known Laura?"

Micah's luminous brown eyes were almost hidden behind her thick curly bangs. She brushed her bangs to the side with her hand. Her light caramel skin was blemish-free except for a mole above her right eyebrow.

Jo thought of the actress, Zendaya, who B.J. seemed to have a crush on despite only being six years old.

Micah answered quietly, "Since middle school. We became friends during dance class."

"What type of dance?"

"Jazz."

Jo nodded. "Let's see, you're attending the

University of North Carolina...UNC, right? How often did you talk to Laura seeing as you were both attending rival colleges?"

Micah smiled slightly. "Not much. We haven't really been in touch until this summer. She called me in June to have lunch with her and asked me to be in her wedding next summer. It was a silly promise from middle school that we would be bridesmaids in each other's weddings. I was really surprised she remembered."

"That's true friendship. Funny thing though, I've heard there was someone else in Laura's life besides Matt."

Micah's eyes widened. "No, I don't think so. They've been together since high school. Every time I was around Laura, all she talked about was wedding plans even though the wedding wasn't until next summer. I know she wanted to graduate first."

"What about Matt? He's finished with school."

"Matt graduated last summer from UNC. He was working here in Charlotte at his dad's construction company. But I think Laura said he got a new job with Ridgecrest Construction. She said he seemed happier not having to work at his dad's company. They weren't getting along."

Jo squinted. "So Matt has some family issues. You sure everything was good between Matt and Laura?"

Micah looked at Jo. "I assumed everything was okay. Laura liked to have things in her life perfect even if they really weren't. She didn't want to appear like she had a problem."

Jo made a note before continuing the questions. "Micah, when did you last talk to Laura?"

"Tuesday. Well, we didn't really talk, more like texted. She had called earlier, but I was running some errands for my mom." Micah looked down at her hands. "So she left a text. She wanted to know if we could get together later in the week."

Jo frowned. "Laura's mother thought she was meeting with friends Tuesday night. What happened to those plans?"

"We were all going to meet that night, but Laura wanted to get together another night closer to the weekend. I don't know why she canceled all of a sudden."

"Who were we?"

"Sarah and me. I guess Reece. Laura seemed to become friends with her again."

"Again?"

Micah shrugged, "They had some kind of falling

out in high school. I guess they made up. To be honest, it was kind of awkward having Reece around."

"Why?"

"She's just not a nice person, always cynical and sarcastic, but…" Micah held her head down causing her thick hair to fall across her face again.

"Micah, continue what you were going to say."

Micah moved her hair. "I don't want to say anything bad about Laura because she was a good friend, but she was mean to other people sometimes. She was a bit of a bully in school."

Jo observed Micah. "Really? Do you think Laura did something to someone in particular recently?"

Micah held up her head and looked directly at Jo. "I don't know. I'm just saying she wasn't liked as much as she thought she was. Sarah and I always told her she should tone it down some. She said what was on her mind, but she wasn't the most sensitive person either. Anyways she had this way about her, people either really loved or hated her."

In her line of work Jo knew being mean and insensitive to the wrong person could cost one to lose her life. Sounded like Laura had that same brash attitude her father was known to have as well. Senator Finney had made quite a few of his own enemies. Jo had a sinking feeling that finding a suspect was going to be increasingly harder to do.

Chapter 9

Monday, August 24 at 3:05 pm

Jo scribbled down notes as Reece strolled in the office. She looked up to watch as the young woman approached. Reece stared back at Jo as though to challenge why she was asked to come. The young woman sat and placed her hands together in her lap.

Jo noticed Reece's fingers were all adorned with a variety of silver rings and black nail polish. Out of the three girls, Reece did seem the least likely to be friends with Laura. She hoped Reece would spill a little more about Laura Finney than the other two young women.

"Reece, thanks for your time. Tell us, how did you know Laura?"

"I have known Laura since elementary school,

I guess. We were best friends back then. Laura, Sarah and me."

Jo raised an eyebrow. "Were you not still friends?"

Reece stared. "Laura and I haven't been friendly for a few years, most of high school. We hung out with different crowds."

"But you have become friends recently?"

"I wouldn't say that. Sarah and I have always been cool. I was not trying to be Laura's BFF. I didn't trust her. And I knew she was suddenly being friendly with me to protect herself."

Jo leaned forward. "What would make Laura want to protect herself?"

Reece smirked. "She didn't want her boyfriend...oh, I mean, fiancé to know she was seeing someone else."

Pete had remained quiet giving his thoughts in between questioning the other young women. He stood from behind the desk and walked closer to Reece, "Sounds more like you had something over Laura's head. Were you blackmailing her or something?"

Reece rolled her eyes. "Now why would I do that?"

Jo cleared her throat to get Pete's attention. She

didn't want Pete antagonizing the young woman. They needed to know what else Reece knew. He turned and looked at her, but remained standing with his arms crossed.

Great, going Pete! Jo took a breath and turned to Reece. "Who was the guy?"

Reece peered up at Pete as if she wanted to run. "I don't know."

"Reece, look at me. I'm assuming you saw Laura with someone that was clearly not her fiancé. What did he look like? Keep in mind, we are investigating Laura's murder. So if you know something, tell us."

Reece's stoic face faltered, but she composed herself. She glared at Jo. "Earlier this summer I saw her at the club where I bartend. She was with a guy I had never seen before. He seemed older, maybe late twenties or even early thirties. He had dark hair, slim build. Not bad-looking. Laura was pretty tall and this guy was definitely taller because when I saw her, she was looking up at him laughing."

Jo noted the description matched the one Sarah gave them earlier. She needed more information. "Anything else?"

Reece shook her head. "I saw her a few days later after that night at Starbucks and I asked her was she still with Matt Vaynor. I really didn't care. I just wanted to see what she would say. She was so smug about herself."

"Anyway, you should have seen her looking all flustered when she showed me her engagement ring. It was a big beautiful diamond, but I know what I saw. So I asked about the guy. She played it off as if he was someone she just met that night, but I could tell she must have liked him because her cheeks turned red. That conversation must have bothered her because a week later I received an invite for the first time in years to the Finneys' annual July 4th party. I haven't been since I was in middle school."

That's interesting. "Could you identify the man you saw Laura with? Did Laura share his name or where he worked?"

Reece shook her head. "I definitely don't know his name. It's been about two months ago now. I may be able to and he may have been back to the club. I'm slinging out drinks from behind the bar all night, so I'm not always paying attention to people unless they're regulars."

Pete asked, "Well, how do you know Laura was seeing him?"

"I can't confirm it was the same guy, but I overheard Laura and Sarah arguing the last time we were out. Sarah is Matt's cousin. I could tell Sarah was upset. She told Laura if she didn't stop seeing this guy she was going to tell Matt. I just assumed it was the same guy from the club earlier this summer. If it wasn't the same guy, Laura was sneaking around seeing some man and Sarah wasn't happy about it."

Jo asked, "How long ago was Laura's argument with Sarah?"

Reece looked thoughtful. "Maybe two weeks ago."

Jo made a note to talk to Sarah again. Someone had to have seen and known more about this elusive man. Next to Matt Vaynor, the mystery man in Laura's life was a definite suspect.

She looked at Reece's hands and noticed she was twisting them.

Jo took a breath. "Reece, you don't need to be nervous. I just have one more question for you. Did Laura reach out to you on Tuesday?"

Reece looked at them. Her cheeks grew red. "Yeah. I'm not sure why she contacted me. I was really getting tired of hanging with them. I did a few times just to see if Laura had changed any."

"Changed?"

Reece sighed. "Like I said, I didn't trust her.

Laura liked to play jokes on people or she was one of those people who liked to spread rumors. It's why we stopped being friends. She basically made people think I was some slut just because a guy she liked had asked me out. Laura was jealous and couldn't believe that someone would even like me. I'm sorry something happened to her, but as far as I'm concerned Laura Finney still thought she was better than everyone else. She seemed to have gotten worse since she was in high school."

Just as Jo concluded when she first saw the young woman, Reece would have no problem telling what she really thought about Laura Finney. "What did Laura and you talk about when she called Tuesday?"

"We didn't really talk. She mainly left messages. She left a text message around three o'clock to say she wanted to meet later in the week. Like I said, I really didn't want to hang out so I was glad she cancelled."

"You said messages. Did she contact you again?"

Reece nodded. "It was a text message the second time too. Look." Reece pulled out her phone and tapped on the screen a few times. She held her phone towards Jo. Jo stood and looked at Reece's face first. Her face turned red again. She appeared embarrassed and shaken.

Jo peered down at the phone. The text message read.

HELP!

At first Jo stared at the screen trying to comprehend. "Laura asked for help?"

Reece stuttered. "I thought she was joking."

"Why did you think she was joking?" Jo snapped.

"I told you she liked to play jokes on people. Why would she contact me of all people if she was in trouble? Besides I wasn't the only one on the message."

Jo frowned. "It's a group message. Who else received it?"

Reece swallowed and peered down, "I recognize Sarah and Micah's phone numbers."

Jo blew out a breath, threw her notebook on the chair and strode towards the door. She flung the door open and looked out into the great room. Most of the crowd had left. She saw no signs of Sarah or Micah. How come neither girl mentioned Laura's very last group text message?

She turned around to see Pete and Reece

looking at her. Jo asked, "What time did that text message come in?"

Reece looked at her phone. "11:18 p.m."

Jo thought about Reece's strange question earlier about needing lawyers. "Did you three talk to each other about this message?"

Reece nodded. "Sarah thought it was best not to say anything. I mean it wasn't like any of us could have helped her. She didn't tell us where she was going. Plus, her parents and Matt thought she was with us. Sarah and Micah were used to covering for Laura. They assumed if her parents or Matt called, they were to say she was with us. I knew nobody was calling me. Mrs. Finney definitely doesn't like me and is probably as puzzled as I am about why Laura was friendly again."

Jo blew out a breath. Now, she was shaking. Out of the three girls she talked to today, she'd thought Sarah would have been the closest friend to Laura. Each one of the young women that were supposed to be Laura's friends had what seemed like strained friendships with the victim. So much so, when she reached out for help, none of them responded. Nor did they acknowledge they knew Laura was in trouble. At the least, one of them could have called 9-1-1 to get the ball rolling to find Laura.

With what information they had gathered, Laura Finney was one complicated young woman. Jo needed to study Laura's phone records and whatever the CSI tech could find on Laura's computer. To successfully solve this case, it was crucial they find out where and with whom Laura had spent her final hours.

Chapter 10

Jo's frustration with the investigation was growing by the hour. Matt Vaynor had become a priority. Jo had left specific instructions at the memorial service to talk to any of those close to Laura. Laura's fiancé seemed to have disappeared since yesterday. Nobody had or wanted to admit they had knowledge of where the young man went after he left the services.

"He's looking real guilty to me," Pete growled as they returned to the office after visiting Matt's parents' house and then to the only residential address they had. The man who answered the door said he had moved in three weeks ago.

Pete raged, "His parents just happened to not

93

have their own son's most recent address. He probably hadn't changed it on the job yet either."

Jo sighed, "Well, Micah was the one who mentioned that Matt didn't get along with his parents, his dad especially. We can check his job and I suspect, Sarah may know. From the interviews, she seemed protective of him with them being cousins."

Pete shook his head and swallowed a swig of coffee. "We can only hope. Sarah should still come in as well as that Reece gal and try to give us something on this mystery guy."

"I agree. They seemed to be talking about the same guy." Jo had to admit she was really keen to talk to Matt Vaynor though. If he'd found out that Laura really wasn't ready for a marriage, he could have reacted badly in anger.

Jo's anger still stirred just thinking about Bryan's transgression, though the affair was only one time as he claimed. Jo rubbed her stiff neck. She didn't need Bryan and her marriage to interfere with this investigation. She got up from her desk chair and walked over to look at the evidence board.

Matt's disappearing act was a sign of guilt, but Matt wasn't the only person of interest. Laura's mystery guy described by both Sarah and Reece was high on the list as well. Jo was disturbed they didn't have more to go on. This man had made himself available once when Sarah and Laura were running a few weeks ago, so it was possible he could have been stalking Laura. Jo had grown weary of coincidences from witnessing people's behaviors during a homicide.

An officer walked towards Jo. "Here are the phone records."

"Thanks, Sgt. Wu. Please keep me updated if you find anything on that laptop."

Sgt. Wu asked, "Is there anything in particular I should look for?"

"Yeah, there's a mystery guy in Laura's life. She had to correspond with him either by phone, email or even social media. See if you can find someone fitting our description."

"Will do, Detective Reed."

Jo started to correct Sgt. Wu. Most of the department knew her when she was Detective Reed only. She added the hyphen and Powell after she married Bryan. Most of the time, she didn't correct anyone and wasn't sure why the way Sgt. Wu addressed her bothered her now.

Jo sat at her desk, grabbed a pencil and studied the numbers on Laura's phone records. The messages Laura sent to her friends were around 11:18 p.m. last Tuesday night. According to the medical examiner, Laura was killed between midnight and sometime early in the morning on Wednesday. There was no more activity on her phone since those last messages to friends who clearly didn't think it was necessary to respond.

So Laura knew she was in trouble sometime after 11:00 p.m. But where was she?

There was one phone call that caught Jo's interest. At 10:08 p.m, Laura answered a call from someone that lasted almost ten minutes. It was a number Laura called and received calls from often. After further search, Jo blinked at her finding.

She called over to Pete. "Hey, this is interesting. Laura received a call from her fiancé after ten o' clock that Tuesday night."

Pete rolled his chair from his desk and peered at her. "Really?"

"They talked for almost ten minutes. This would have been almost an hour before she sent out her message to her friends."

She sat back in her seat. "Let's think this through. Laura was out possibly with another man. It looks like Matt called quite a few times. So she's ignoring her fiancé's phone calls and finally picks up. I wonder how that conversation went. She certainly didn't reach out to him for help when she texted her friends."

Pete answered, "He could have been the one she needed to get away from. I just found out some interesting things about Matt Vaynor too. Come look at this."

Jo walked over to Pete's desk and leaned down to look at his computer screen.

Peter pointed to the monitor. "This guy has a record. He has some DUIs and assault and battery charges from three years ago. Apparently he got into a fight with a guy at a club. According to this, Matt claimed he was defending his girlfriend. So some guy messed with Laura and Matt went berserk."

Jo frowned, "The jealous type. I wonder how much the Finneys approved of this engagement. Or was Laura still engaged? Remember, she left her engagement ring at home that night. We don't know why. It could have been that the engagement was off or she just didn't want this guy she was out with to know she was engaged to another man."

The more Jo thought about it, if the engagement was off, Laura hadn't cleared up any other reminders of Matt. There was still the wallpaper photo of the happy couple on Laura's laptop.

Pete pulled a map off of his desk and walked over to the evidence board. "We have a few motives building for either of these guys. Check this out. Let's just say Matt did find out his fiancée was cheating on him."

Pete pinned the map on the board and then circled an area of the map with a red pen. "Laura's body was found in this vicinity behind Pine Woods Park Apartments. The last location on her phone was here." Pete marked another location on the map. "There are apartment complexes as well as a few residential areas. This area in particular is a mile away from where her body was found, and guess who lives here now?"

Jo blew out a breath. "Matt? This is his new place?"

Pete tilted his head. "Just confirmed with a college buddy of his. They helped him move in three weeks ago."

She crossed her arms. "If he killed Laura, why would he dump his fiancée's body that close to him?"

Pete shrugged, "Looks like she talked to him on the phone. Who's to say she didn't go see him, they argued. It ended badly. He might have just wanted to get her out of his apartment. Come on, this guy has been hiding. If he wanted to help us, he would have at least showed up for us to talk to him."

This seemed almost too easy. So many times it was the spouse or boyfriend, but something bothered Jo. She examined the photo with the ligatures around Laura's neck. They originally thought the crime seemed similar to Maddock's m.o., and that Laura's murder could have been a copycat. Hopefully, that wasn't the case.

"We need to talk to Matt Vaynor, even if we have to drag him in here. We're also going to need a search warrant for his apartment. I'll get started on paperwork."

Jo sat at her desk. They needed to get some real leads and start building this case against someone soon. Any day now, Jo was confident Senator Finney was going to come at them with some heat about his daughter's murder.

She wanted to be ready.

Chapter 11

Tuesday, August 25 at 3:45 pm

Jo and Pete stepped off the elevator onto the third floor and entered through the double glass doors marked Ridgecrest Construction. A woman with long reddish wavy hair that hung down her back was on the phone. Jo made eye contact with the woman who smiled and lifted her finger to let them know she would be with them soon. Jo looked around the office. She noticed a conference room nearby where a group of people was talking. Matt Vaynor wasn't at his apartment. They were here to see if anyone at his job had seen him.

The woman hung up the phone. Behind her round brown glasses, her green eyes blinked, showing off long black lashes. "Sorry for the wait. How may I help you?"

Jo pulled out her badge. "I'm Detective Jo Reed-Powell and this is my partner Detective Pete McConnelly. Is Matt Vaynor in the office today?"

"Oh my. Is this about his Laura? I've seen the news. It's so sad. Matt came in this morning, even though we all told him to stay home. He may have gone home already, but I'm not sure. I'll show you his office."

Jo looked at Pete. Both his eyebrows shot up in the air. This was really unexpected. So maybe the young man wasn't hiding out as they suspected.

They followed the petite redhead who was even shorter than Jo down a hallway past several offices and stopped in front of an office across from the copier. The door was closed. "We understood if he needed time, but he came in this morning. He looked horrible, so I hope he did go home. Here's his office."

"Thank you." Pete stepped in front of the woman and knocked on the door before opening it.

A man looked up surprised. He'd been looking through a folder he had in his hands. Jo stared at him thinking he looked familiar to her. He was definitely not the man Jo remembered seeing on

Laura's laptop wallpaper. He kind of looked like a taller version of the guy who played Harry Potter.

Pete asked, "Matt Vaynor?"

The man pushed his glasses up on his nose and shook his head. "No, I'm Matt's co-worker. Josh Collins. You are?"

Pete and Jo displayed their badges.

"Oh! You must be here to talk about Laura. Matt and I were having a meeting. He should be back soon. Poor guy. He needed to compose himself." Josh held out the folder in his hand. "I told him this project could wait and he should go home."

Behind them a man spoke. His voice was hoarse. "Hello?"

Jo spun around to see the man who had entered the office. *Now this was Matt.* Dressed in a blue shirt and khakis, Matt's athletic body filled out his clothes. All the glorious blond hair he had in the picture on Laura's laptop was gone, replaced with a buzz cut. Jo could tell by his bloodshot eyes that the young man had experienced a few difficult days and nights. They needed to determine if guilt was mixed in with the grief. "I presume you're Matt Vaynor?"

He nodded and then answered, "Yes. You two look like detectives."

It wasn't often anyone described her as looking like a detective. Jo found it interesting that Matt assumed so, like he had been expecting them. They had only been trying to track him down for days.

From behind, Josh spoke, "Matt, don't worry about this. I can handle the project from here."

Matt looked frustrated. "Are you sure? I really could use something to do."

Josh walked over to pat Matt on the shoulder. "Take it one day at a time, son."

Jo watched Josh leave. The man didn't appear to be that much older than Matt, but he spoke to Matt like he was his dad.

Matt walked back behind his desk. "You want to sit?"

Pete responded, "No thanks. This shouldn't take too long. We're sorry for your loss. We understand this is a difficult time."

Matt rubbed his face. He had a beard growing in what was past the five o'clock shadow phase. "I still can't believe any of this."

Jo spoke up. "Mr. Vaynor, we talked to some of Laura's friends at the memorial service. We missed you."

"You can call me Matt. Sounds like you're referring to my dad when you talk to me like that.

Sorry, I couldn't stay. I had to get out of there. All of those people expressing their condolences. I just can't process that she's gone."

"We understand. Can you tell us about the last time you talked to Laura?"

Matt didn't look up. He seemed to struggle for an answer. "Maybe Tuesday? I've been pulling long hours at work."

"So you talked to her Tuesday night?"

"Yeah, when I got off work I called her a few times. She didn't answer so I called my cousin thinking they were together. Sarah told me Laura had made other plans."

"But you did eventually talk to Laura?" Jo asked.

Matt's face seemed to grow white in front of them.

Jo looked at Pete. "Are you okay, Matt?"

His eyes appeared vacant as if he was trying to remember something. "Yes, we talked. Or rather, I should say we argued."

Jo inquired, "About?"

"She wouldn't tell me where she was."

"Okay, so you argued for how long?"

"I don't know. A few minutes. She hung up on me."

Pete asked, "Where were you Tuesday night after midnight?"

Jo thought she saw fear in Matt's eyes. Matt swallowed. "I don't think I can talk to you anymore."

Pete asked, "Why?"

Matt looked at them. "Because I think I need my lawyer."

Pete looked at me. "Are you sure?"

"Yes, I need to call my lawyer."

Pete stared at Matt like he wanted to punch him. "Well, Mr. Vaynor, we'll need to finish this downtown since you're not willing to cooperate."

Jo stared at Matt. *Did he do this?* Surely, Matt Vaynor wasn't going to confess to killing his fiancée. *God, could this case finally become that easy.*

In the back of her mind, Jo had a growing sense this case was going to take a turn she wouldn't see coming.

Chapter 12

Tuesday, August 25 at 5:15 pm

They needed to wait for Matt's lawyer to show up. Matt was cooperative about riding back with them and sitting in the interview room. Jo looked at Matt through the mirrored glass. This man clearly had a motive to kill Laura. She hated to admit it, but she understood what would have driven Matt to kill.

She looked up at the clock on the wall and shoved her hands in her pocket. She hated to do it, but she had to call home. Jo walked back to her desk and dialed her home phone. She cringed as Bryan answered. "I'm just touching base to say I will be late."

Bryan responded back slowly as if he was

thinking as he spoke. "We're good here. I guess we'll see you later then."

Jo didn't like Bryan's tone. It was as if he was numb to her calling about being late. She looked at the phone before hanging up. Really, she had kept a pretty good schedule for most of the year. It was just this recent case that had thrown her off.

The thought of her and Bryan heading towards divorce didn't sit well in her spirit. They both loved B.J. fiercely and all Jo could picture was a bitter custody battle. More than she wanted to admit, especially now and in the last year, Jo was often the absent parent. It was crucial to check out every lead when it came to solving a case and that took time.

Jo leaned back in her seat, closed her eyes and rubbed her pounding temples as her mother's words rang in her ears. *Pray! Trust God to guide you, Josephine.*

Pete tapped on her desk, "Jo, Mr. Vaynor's lawyer is here. This guy has got to be guilty. He has one of the best defense lawyers in Charlotte."

"What?"

Jo snatched her notebook off of her desk and marched towards the interview room. She noticed a familiar face indeed. Adam Locklear was the kind of lawyer you called when you were in real trouble.

Not many lawyers were cheap, but not just anyone could afford Adam Locklear. Jo couldn't wait to mention to Asia about this one. Adam had dated Asia several years ago and he seemed like the one who would finally reel Asia into marriage. That didn't happen mainly because her older sister was just as stubborn and strong willed as Adam Locklear.

One thing for sure, Jo doubted they would get a confession from Matt Vaynor. She walked in the room and faced the two men. Matt wouldn't look up. Jo thought if this man was trying to appear innocent, he wasn't doing a very good job.

Adam grinned as if he hit the jackpot. "Detective Reed, how good to see you again. It's been awhile."

This wasn't a social call. "Yes, it has Mr. Locklear. It's Detective Reed-Powell. Thanks." Jo usually didn't correct most people about her name, but Adam was a special case and she didn't want him to think he had the upper hand at all.

Jo sat. "Matt, we sure would love to get to the bottom of what happened to Laura. Don't you think we owe Laura's parents the truth?"

Silence.

Jo tapped her pen on the table. They were past

being nice to the grieving fiancé. "Mr. Vaynor, can you please tell us where you were on Tuesday night after midnight?"

She watched as Matt looked at his lawyer. Adam nodded as if to give Matt permission to speak.

"I went driving around."

Jo leaned forward. "I assume by yourself or wait, maybe Laura was with you."

Matt said fast, "No, she wasn't with me. I was driving around because I was upset. I had been trying to call her. Sarah told me they were not together and I wanted to know where she was. She wouldn't answer my calls."

Jo questioned, "But she did finally answer." She looked at her notes for reference, "Around 10:08 p.m. Would you say that's about the time you and Laura had your argument?"

Matt looked at Jo, but didn't say anything.

Jo continued. "You talked a full ten minutes. I assume that conversation really set you off because at some point you realized Laura was out with another man."

Matt flinched as if Jo hit him. He looked at his lawyer.

Adam shook his head. "Come on, Detective Reed. That wasn't necessary. If you're going to treat my client this way, I'll need to stop this questioning."

Jo glared at Adam. "Finding out the person you love is cheating on you can drive a person to do things they wouldn't normally think to do. Isn't that right, Matt?"

Matt shook his head. "She'd been more interested in planning the wedding than me for a while now."

Jo eyed Matt. "So, Laura had been stringing you along for a few months. That had to make you really angry. Angry enough to hurt her. Did you hurt her?"

"No—"

Adam interrupted. "Don't answer that question. Detective, are you accusing Mr. Vaynor of something? Do you have any evidence that would place Laura anywhere near Mr. Vaynor the night of her tragic death?"

Pete snapped, "You tell us. We were having a sympathetic conversation with Mr. Vaynor and he called a lawyer. It's obvious he was upset and apparently he lost track of time, because it's clear he has no alibi."

Jo pulled out the photo of Laura from a folder in front of her.

"We still need to know what you were doing during this time." She pushed the photo closer. "Did you find Laura? Did you do this to her?"

Matt pushed his chair back, staring at the photo of Laura's dead body in horror. He wailed, "Oh God! No! I broke off the engagement. It was over. I was hurt, but..."

Adam turned towards Matt. "Don't say any more." He looked back at Jo and Pete. "My client has lost a woman that meant the world to him. Let's stop this. If you don't have anything, there is no need for you to question him."

Pete leaned in and stated, "He needs to establish where he was around the time of Laura's death."

Jo pushed ahead. "Laura found someone else. That had to make you angry, Matt."

Matt grabbed his head. "I felt like she was out with someone else, but she wouldn't say who. I was angry."

Adam spoke up, "That's enough, Matt."

Matt continued. "I knew she was out with someone else. I didn't want to believe it. She'd been hounding me about getting married for years. I proposed last Christmas, and it's been nothing but talk about the wedding and how there was so much to do by next summer."

Adam tapped the table. "We don't have to continue this discussion. My client just lost his fiancée, his high school sweetheart. Let him grieve."

Jo wasn't finished and recognized Matt wanted to get something off his chest. "Where did you go, Matt?"

Matt blubbered. "I went...drinking. I haven't had a drink in three years. I just went to some bar. I don't remember where. I don't remember how I even got back home. I'd been sober for three years. I didn't know what else to do."

Matt stared at Jo. The intensity in his eyes practically sucked the breath out of her. She felt his pain at being betrayed, but then Jo remembered something that had been bothering her.

Why did Laura suddenly cancel on her friends? Why take the engagement ring off after being so excited about planning a wedding?

Jo looked at Matt. "You didn't break off the engagement with Laura the night she died. Did you? Something happened before. She went out with this guy out of anger with you."

He opened his mouth, but nothing came out. Finally he said, "I messed up. We argued the night before. I was trying to get back with her because I didn't want to lose her. I wasn't faithful either, but I still felt like we should have been together."

Jo felt a deep sense of anger well up in her. "So she broke off the engagement because you were cheating. She decides to go out with some guy she'd been flirting with probably to get you out of her mind. You didn't like it and you wanted her back. If you couldn't get her back, then nobody would have her."

"That's not what happened," Matt shouted.

Jo pointed her finger at Matt. "You better make sure you didn't do this, Mr. Vaynor because you will pay for killing Laura Finney. Let me advise you, you better find out exactly where you were that night."

She got up and left the interview room. If she stayed in there any longer, she might have hit Matt. *Why was it so simple for people to betray the people they supposedly loved?*

Chapter 13

Thursday, August 27 at 2:22 p.m.

Two days had passed since the interview with Matt, and Jo still was disgusted. Her mood about the case clung to her and only worsened when she got home. She couldn't even look at Bryan. The details of this case were working her last nerve.

Jo tried to switch her thinking around and put herself in their shoes. Matt had just turned twenty-three years old and Laura was twenty-one. Jo tried to think about their ages and the fact that they were both young and together for so long. Her mind still kept asking the question, was no one really into having a fully committed relationship anymore? Was marriage just something a couple did, and when things became difficult, it was time to look elsewhere? *What a joke!*

Jo wasn't laughing. Her life as it once was three weeks ago had turned upside down. She didn't know what to do at home, and this case was moving at a snail's pace. If Matt couldn't prove where he was that night, both she and Pete wanted to arrest him though having a motive clearly wasn't enough reason. They'd at least finally received the search warrant early Thursday morning.

Matt had only been living at the Greater Hills Apartment for three weeks. From Jo's walk through earlier, she found boxes still piled up in a second bedroom that Matt had not finished unpacking. The living room and master bedroom were fully furnished. The bedroom had clothes scattered everywhere as if Matt took off his work clothes and left them where they hit the floor. The kitchen had pizza boxes and Chinese take-out spilling out of a trash can in the corner.

The living room was the most orderly room. Almost too orderly compared to the rest of the apartment. Jo moved past CSI as they dusted for prints in the living room. She looked out the window of the second floor apartment. When they turned into the apartment complex, Jo noticed that Pine Woods Park Apartments where Laura's body was found was not that far away. If they traveled down the road another mile, they would arrive at the crime scene.

Jo was still bothered by the closeness. She turned around and looked at the apartment. They needed to know if the original crime scene took place in Matt's apartment. Was it possible Laura realized she should make up with Matt even after she broke off the engagement? Whatever was going through Laura's mind about this new guy, did she still want to plan her perfect wedding? If Laura did come to see Matt that night, Jo tried to think about how Matt would have carried Laura's body out of the apartment. He would have had to make a lot of noise trying to carry or drag her down the flight of stairs.

Beige-colored carpeting was wall-to-wall in the entire apartment. There were no signs of the burgundy-colored fibers that were found on and around Laura. That didn't mean Matt hadn't owned a rug. From the quick look the current owner allowed yesterday at Matt's previous place, there were hardwood floors. *Definitely a place for using rugs.*

Jo walked up towards the kitchen, where Matt stood with his arms crossed leaning on the kitchen counter. He observed Jo warily as she approached him.

"I can't answer questions without my lawyer."

Jo smiled, "I'm sure Mr. Locklear won't mind you cooperating with us. Matt, did you own a rug at one time?"

Matt considered her question for a few seconds before responding. "I had rugs in my previous place. As you can see here I don't need them now."

"What happened to those rugs?" Jo inquired.

Matt shrugged, "I put them in storage."

"Can we get access to your storage?"

"Why?"

Jo tilted her head. "Why do you insist on not helping us with the murder of your fiancée or should I say ex-fiancée?"

Matt un-crossed his arms and stood straight. "You want me to be a suspect?"

Jo wasn't bothered by Matt's menacing stance. "Matt, I want the truth. I want to be able to tell Senator and Mrs. Finney what happened to their daughter. The search warrant covers all your property, so where is that storage facility?"

Matt dropped his shoulders as though he was defeated. "I can take you there. I want to call my lawyer though."

"That's fine. You can ride with us."

Pete drove as Matt provided directions. Jo mentally noted the storage facility was about two miles away from Matt's apartment and three miles from where Laura was found. As Pete pulled into the parking lot, Jo's first thought was these storage units were actually a good place to hide a body. It was sad the way her mind had been trained to think after all of these years in homicide.

They exited the car and followed Matt down a row until they stopped at a storage unit marked 5G. Matt opened the lock and lifted up the door. Like most typical storage units, boxes and furniture were piled high.

Jo stepped inside. "You have a lot of furniture in here, Mr. Vaynor."

He answered. "I had a lot more room in the house. I couldn't fit as much as I wanted into the apartment."

"Why did you move?"

"New job. Not as much pay."

"Didn't you used to work for your father?"

"My dad and I don't get along very well. I was mistaken to think I could work for him."

Pete walked in and starting looking at furniture. "Where are those rugs, Matt?"

Matt frowned. "I think we put them on the truck first so they would have been last. They're piled up over here." Matt walked over to the right side of the storage unit, where rugs lay on top of a dresser.

Jo peered inside the ends of the rolled up rugs. One rug was beige and the other one appeared to be blue. "Are these all of your rugs?"

Matt frowned. "No. One seems to be missing."

Jo exchanged a look with Pete before asking, "Can you describe it?"

"It was the rug I kept in the living room. It had a burgundy and a black pattern over beige. I wonder what happened to it. I know we took everything off the truck. My mother gave me that rug."

Jo asked, "Would you have a picture of it?

Matt turned to Jo. "Why? Why are you so interested in that rug?"

Jo's phone rang. "I have to take this call."

She walked out of the storage unit. "Hello, this is Detective Reed-Powell."

"Detective, this is Officer Emmanuel, I think we found something over here at the apartment."

"What did you find?"

"In the back of the closet in the master bedroom, there was some rope. We bagged it."

"This is good, Officer Emmanuel. Hey, we need

some CSI techs to come to a storage unit about two miles down the road from the apartments."

"Yes, ma'am."

Jo clicked her phone off and walked back towards the storage unit. Matt looked distressed.

He was asking Pete, "Why are you asking about the rug?"

Pete stared Matt down. "Why are you worried?"

"Because I know it must have something to do with Laura. Why else would you ask me? I should have asked my lawyer to come."

Jo observed Matt. "Calm down, Matt. If you didn't do anything, you have no reason to get yourself upset."

She stepped inside the storage unit and examined the other rugs. Each one of the rugs were held together with a rope, probably similar to the same rope the CSI tech just found in Matt's apartment. *Was it like the rope used to strangle Laura?*

There was no doubt in her mind that the missing rug was the same one they found wrapped around Laura's body. Matt Vaynor was looking more and more like their suspect. They had no choice but to arrest him.

Chapter 14

Monday, August 31 at 11:12 p.m.

No one wanted to be in their boss's office first thing Monday morning. After they made the arrest on Thursday, Matt Vaynor's face was splashed on the news and social media throughout the weekend. Even CNN picked up on the story. Senator Finney appeared on camera relaying his shock about his former future son-in-law.

Captain Walter Ransom scanned the report again before looking at them. "So Matt Vaynor made bail this morning. Let's review the evidence. He doesn't have an alibi, had pretty good motive to kill, and CSI found similar rope, which could have been used as the murder weapon. I see you have confirmed the rug found around Laura's body is the same rug owned by Matt Vaynor." The captain sat back and crossed his arms. "Still there are some shaky areas, there is no DNA evidence, and the district attorney is asking for more."

Jo stated. "I agree. Matt Vaynor has already hired Adam Locklear as his defense attorney. We still need to find out where Matt was the night he went binge drinking."

Pete leaned in. "I have talked to some of Matt's buddies. Matt was a mean drunk. Most of his fights started after he'd had way too much to drink."

Jo thought out loud. "Someone hit Laura before she was strangled. There's the bruising on the left side of her face, but as far as we know, there was no previous abuse."

Captain Ransom slapped the desk. "There could have been abuse that was never reported. You guys need to make sure Matt found Laura that night. He had to have gone drinking somewhere. Check any credit card or debit charges he may have made that night. What about this guy that Laura was supposedly out with? Did this date actually happen and if so where? The timeline is still fuzzy, folks."

Jo felt overwhelmed as she left the captain's office. There were still too many missing blanks on the timeline that haunted her all weekend. The more she scoured Laura's phone records, the more she was coming up empty with this other guy. If Laura really went out on a date, she must have had another way of communicating with this guy. She would need to get with Sgt. Wu to see if he was able to retrieve any other information from Laura's laptop.

Since this was going to be a long Monday, she called Bryan. He didn't answer his cell phone so she left a message. "Bryan, I know it's my turn to pick up B.J. This Finney case has become a bit more hectic now, as I know you've seen on the news. I'll be home late tonight. I do have some dinner selections in the freezer."

Jo hung up the phone. She was no cook like her mother, but she learned her way around a slow-cooker on the weekends. She did what she could.

Her desk phone rang. Not sure if it was Bryan or not, Jo let the phone ring twice before answering, "Detective Reed-Powell."

"Tell them to leave him alone."

Jo frowned. "Who is this and leave who alone?"

"It's me, Sarah Anderson, Laura's friend and Matt's cousin. You talked to me at Laura's memorial service. Why are you trying to blame Matt? He couldn't have killed Laura."

Couldn't have killed, Jo thought. She responded,

"We're doing our jobs, Sarah." Jo recalled those interviews. "Are you covering for Matt since he is your cousin?"

"What are you talking about? Matt didn't do anything to Laura. Laura was my best friend."

"Why didn't you mention that she reached out to you all for help?"

Sarah sucked in a breath. "Look, I felt awful. I'm not a bad person. I was mad with her and I really didn't take her seriously. I figured she probably just wanted to get out of her date, which she shouldn't have been on in the first place. She was engaged!"

"Did you know she broke off the engagement with Matt because she found out *he* was cheating on her?"

Sarah was silent for a moment. "I didn't know that. I just know Matt was calling her over and over again. Then he called me because he thought we were together. He was frantic and really worried about her."

Jo thought for a second. "So let me guess, you told Matt that Laura could have been on a date with someone. Didn't you? He talked to you and asked you why you all didn't go out, so you had to tell him something."

"Yes, I told him. Okay, they both didn't know

what they wanted. They had broken up so many times over the years, dating other people, but they always got back together. Laura told me just a few weeks ago how much she loved Matt and that they'd been together so long she felt like they should get married. That's not a reason to get married, but they seemed like they were made for each other."

"Have you known Matt to be violent towards Laura?"

"Never. He did stupid stuff, but he would never lay a hand on her."

"Well, Sarah, if you want to help Matt, you need to tell me more about this other guy. Right now, Matt is our focus and he doesn't know where he was the night Laura was killed."

Sarah cried out, "I know where Matt was that night."

Jo's hand tightened on the phone. "Are you about to tell me the truth or is this your way of just helping out your cousin? I would be careful, Sarah."

"I'm telling you the truth. When Matt called me, I asked him where he was. It took me awhile to figure out what he was saying, but I realized he went to one of his old hangouts. I ordered Uber, found Matt, took his car keys and drove him back to his place."

Jo's heart sank. If Sarah was telling the truth, then Matt had an alibi. "This is awfully convenient that you're coming forward now."

"I didn't know Matt couldn't remember to tell you. I just found out after seeing my cousin's face plastered all over the news that you're trying to pin Laura's death on him. He was barely able to stand and walk that night. He hadn't been drinking in years. I went by his place this morning because I was really worried about him and wanted him to call his sponsor. He's devastated. I'm still hoping I can get him to go to an AA meeting."

Jo sighed. She couldn't feel sorry for Matt. He wasn't the victim. "What time did you pick Matt up the night of August 18th?"

"Wow, that seems so long ago now even though it's been a few weeks. I believe it was close to midnight when the Uber driver dropped me off at Nick's Place. That's the name of the bar."

Jo wrote down the name of the bar. They would need to get an arrival time for Matt. She didn't like this at all. This was just too convenient and they had evidence connected to Matt.

Suppose Sarah had something to do with Laura's death too?

"What time did you get Matt home?"

"I think I drove Matt back to his place around one o'clock in the morning. I had to drive around awhile because I couldn't figure out how to get to his new apartment. When I finally remembered, it felt like it took forever to get him up those stairs to his apartment. I was so exhausted. I slept on his couch and left before he woke up. My roommate picked me up that morning so you can ask her."

Jo shook her head. *This is not looking good.* Still, they only had Sarah's word and how reliable was this young woman right now? They would soon find out.

Sarah cleared her throat. "There is something else you should know. I may have seen the guy Laura was sneaking around with again."

Jo sat very still. "Where did you see him?"

Sarah answered with a slight tremor in her voice. "I said I may have. I'm not sure if it was him. He looked the same, but different. Different haircut, maybe. And I could be wrong."

Jo's nerves felt like someone had lit a match and set her on fire. "Sarah, think carefully. Where were you when you *think* you saw him?"

"I thought I saw him this morning when I was leaving Matt's apartment. He was getting out of a black car. It may have been a Honda, but I'm not sure. I'm no car expert. Anyway, this guy looked directly at me like he recognized me. His eyes gave me the creeps. I kept thinking, where have I seen him before? Then it occurred to me this could be same guy I saw with Laura when we were out running a month ago. Like I said, he looked different."

Something stirred inside of Jo causing her stomach to feel upset. Why would Sarah think she saw this man near Matt's apartment? Did the man live there? Did he know Matt? "Did this man go towards Matt's apartment?"

"I don't know. Someone was honking their horn a few apartments down. I turned for like a few seconds. But when I looked back, the guy was gone. Maybe I can ask Matt about him, but that would be crazy. Laura wouldn't have gone out with someone that Matt knew. She wasn't that stupid." Sarah laughed in an uncomfortable way as if the thought brought her pain. "I could be confused, you know. There are a lot of creepy guys out there."

"Thanks for your help, Sarah."

If this was the same guy, they need to find him

fast. Jo jotted down "black Honda" on her pad. Searching for the car would be beyond looking for a needle in a haystack, but it was something. Now looking for a creepy guy who drove a black car and who *may* know Matt would definitely narrow the search. Jo wrote Matt's name down and circled it.

Matt may have an alibi, but Jo felt like he was still involved in Laura's death.

Chapter 15

Monday, August 31 at 9:05 p.m.

Jo drove down I-77, her thoughts on the Laura Finney case. Sarah coming forward with an alibi for Matt meant they had to make a statement to the media. Dropping charges against Matt would not keep Senator Finney from throwing a fit, so they still had to find a suspect. Pete and she both agreed the number one priority was to find the man Laura was seeing on the side.

Pete threw out a bunch of crazy theories, "Maybe Matt and this guy were working together? Who's to say Sarah and Matt weren't working together? Sarah didn't seem to be that much of a best friend to Laura."

Jo was deeply disturbed that Sarah thought she saw the man near Matt's apartment. Suppose someone was trying to set Matt up? That seemed crazy to Pete, but Jo kept thinking about certain details they had found around Matt. Matt said a lot of people helped him pack up his things before moving. The rope was used to bind furniture and those rugs. Then there was the missing rug from the storage facility that was wrapped around Laura's body. There was no evidence a crime took place in Matt's apartment. There were too many details and some of them seemed to conveniently point to Matt as the obvious suspect.

But who would want to hurt Laura and place the blame on Matt? That meant the man Laura was with had to have known Matt.

Jo stopped thinking long enough to focus on the exit signs and noticed she needed to change into the right lane soon. She wouldn't be able to switch her mind off from the case for long especially when she got in bed to go to sleep. She still had trouble sleeping for the past few nights. In between throwing around thoughts about the case, she wondered if she was going down the same road as her partner. Pete barely had a relationship with his kids and from the way he talked, he may not be walking down the aisle with wife number three. His girlfriend broke up with him last weekend.

Jo pulled into the garage. She hated arriving home this late, but what could she do? As she climbed out of the car and headed to the side door, she felt like she was earning an award for being the worst mother. She hadn't seen B.J. since morning and she knew Bryan had tucked him into bed. They had agreed to have B.J. in bed by seven-thirty on school nights.

The house was silent when Jo entered. As she walked past the guest bedroom, she could hear the television through the crack in the door. She started to knock, but kept walking towards B.J.'s room. She opened the door. B.J. insisted on sleeping with a light on so they had night lights plugged in on two sides of the room. Jo walked over and looked down at her son. Her eyes watered. This case was starting to feel like the months she'd spent on the Maddock case. Since the beginning of the year, Jo liked being able to pick up her baby boy from school or from her parents' home, get dinner ready and tuck him into bed.

She hadn't been able to do any of those things for quite a few days now.

Jo bent and kissed her son on the forehead. "Sorry, B.J. I'll be sure to fix you a nice breakfast in the morning." As soon as she said it, she was reminded that Bryan fixed breakfast again this morning. He'd adjusted something with work. He seemed to keep way better hours than she did right now. Bryan was the better parent, which made it even harder on Jo's psyche.

She walked out of B.J.'s room towards the bedroom. Jo turned on the lamp by her side of the bed and unbuttoned her shirt. She kicked off her shoes and fell back on the bed. She was bone-tired, but not so weary that the loneliness of the bedroom didn't settle on her like it did every night.

Lord, how is my life supposed to continue like this?

Jo heard a knock at the door and lifted her head. Bryan stood in the doorway. *Well, God, you answered that one fast.* Judging by the grim expression on Bryan's face, she knew this would be a difficult conversation. She prayed for the strength to handle it.

Jo lifted her body to a sitting position. "I hope you received my message."

Bryan nodded. "I did. B.J. was really upset tonight. I had a hard time getting him to go to bed. He wanted to wait up for you."

That pierced Jo's heart. "I've been upsetting him a lot lately."

"We've both been guilty. The question is what are we going to do?"

Jo stared at Bryan. "You mean about us?"

"Yes. I know what you do as a homicide detective is really important. It's a gritty job and someone has to do it. You're good at your job. Last year, I saw you become obsessed with that case. You were really not here. A lot."

Jo remained silent. She knew she'd been missing in action. Bryan didn't say anything. Most of the time, he didn't have to. She could see the disappointment on his face and especially on B.J.'s face.

Bryan walked into the room and sat on the bench by the closet. "Don't take this the wrong way. I made some mistakes that I'm responsible for, but Jo we...B.J. needs you. I watched the news over the weekend. Before you even called and left your message, I saw the coverage of this Matt guy. People are questioning if he killed the senator's daughter. I know that's your case."

Jo looked away from Bryan and rubbed her head. "Well, Matt Vaynor has an alibi now. This is not like the Maddock case. That was a serial killer that had to be stopped."

"But you're spending as much time on this case.

I expected by now you wanted to talk about...you know."

"Your affair?" Jo blew out a breath. "What's done is done. You broke my trust."

"Do you still want to be married, Jo? I feel like you've already made a decision, but you haven't said it out loud. You're just going on with your work as usual."

"I haven't decided anything. Are you saying you want a divorce? Is it what you want?"

Bryan stared at her. "Is that what you're thinking about?"

Jo stood from the bed ignoring her tired body. "I didn't marry you ever planning to divorce you. I would have never imagined you would cheat on me either. I think about our marriage all the time. I'm praying about what I should I do. I'll be the first to admit, I'm also distracted right now. Maybe I want to be distracted because I'm hurt."

Bryan stretched his arms out. "I'm so sorry I hurt you. We can't just stay the way we are either. If you get another case, where you get obsessed again, I don't know if I can handle that. I have a feeling this case has already crossed over that line for you."

Jo tilted her head to the side. "What are you saying?"

"I'm saying I don't think I can stay in a marriage where my wife disappears and gets lost in her work. I don't want to ever put myself in that position, where I'm tempted again."

She crossed her arms. "So, it's my fault? Are you asking me to give up my career so you won't be tempted to run into the arms of another woman?"

"I'm not asking you to give up anything, Jo. I'm asking you to remember you are a wife and a mother."

Jo yelled, "How can you say that? I never forget you and B.J. Just like I never forget when I see someone dead that they're someone's spouse, mother or father, a brother or a sister. I always remember how I would feel if I lost someone close to me."

Jo sank back down on the bed. "If you're this unhappy, you do what you need to do, Bryan. I'm doing the best I can right now. I supported you when you struggled. I just really didn't expect you to go this route."

Bryan responded, "B.J. needed you tonight, not me. He wanted his mother. I remember how you talked about your dad not always being there when you were growing up. I just wanted you to know B.J. can relate."

Fear pierced her heart as she watched Bryan walk away. She felt like her marriage was a losing battle. If she wasn't careful, she would lose her son. Jo was not about to let that happen.

Chapter 16

Thursday, September 3 at 9:39 a.m.

Jo and Bryan had not talked anymore after Bryan openly confessed he could not take her growing obsession with another case. For the past two days, Jo's investigation of Laura Finney's death had taken a slow dive of no progress, despite the captain's daily veiled threats. This morning, the weight of Bryan's words sunk in as Jo realized the case had taken a drastic turn in a direction she could have never seen coming. A little over two weeks after finding Laura Finney's body, they had another murder scene.

Jo looked down at Sarah's body. A mixture of shock and fear coursed through her. Sarah was found in her home with her wrists bound behind her. Jo found herself not being able to focus. Her mind raced backwards to the Maddock case. Sarah's death appeared to almost match Maddock's m.o.

Is someone playing some sick game here?

Jo glanced at Pete. He looked as grave as she felt. She shifted her eyes to Lou as he walked and recorded notes. Jo held her hand to her head as if it would keep her from losing her mind. What she needed to do was separate all of the other crime scenes in her head and focus solely on this one. Jo tried to recreate the scene inside her head.

Sarah had struggled. She didn't just let her assailant inside. Jo imagined someone caught the young woman off guard as she entered her house. A scuffle ensued in the hallway. The lamp on the table was knocked over. Sarah's purse had been flung against a wall. All the items were scattered everywhere. She must have been attacked from behind holding mail in her hand because envelopes and a magazine were strewn across the floor. She had no idea how long Sarah was tied up. The ligatures around her neck indicated strangulation was most likely the cause of death.

Just three days ago, Jo had listened on the phone as the young woman begged them to leave her cousin alone. She provided an alibi for Matt that Jo and Pete had since confirmed with the Uber driver, Sarah's roommate and the bartender at Nick's Place. Matt was no longer a suspect, but he was still connected.

Pete looked at Jo and nodded to his right. "Not-so lucky for him having to find her and call it in. Still thinking he's not involved?"

Jo looked at Pete. "This is someone else. Sarah cleared Matt. She was his alibi. What would have been his motive?"

Jo swung around and looked at Matt who sat on the stairs weeping openly. Jo could not deny she felt bad for him. First, his fiancée and now his cousin. Matt had told them Sarah's roommate was out-of-town, and was having a hard time getting in touch with Sarah. Matt drove over to the house to check on his cousin.

Jo walked over to Matt and crouched.

Through his tears, Matt moaned. "Sarah always looked out for me."

Jo sympathized, "I'm so sorry, Matt. Had you and Sarah talked since Monday? Did she mention a man to you? He would've been tall with dark hair. Do you know someone who fits that description that would have come to see you Monday?"

Matt shook his head. "What? Nobody came to

see me on Monday but Sarah." He stuttered through tears. "I haven't talked to Sarah since Monday."

Jo turned and walked back towards Pete. "Sarah must have found this guy. She got too close to him. He knew she'd made a connection to him and Laura. This was about keeping Sarah quiet."

Pete smirked, "So we're still trying to track down the mystery guy we can't seem to find. The captain is going to want to strangle us."

Jo thought for a minute. "There was one other person who saw this guy. We need to talk to her and this time she needs to give us something we can use. Sarah was her friend too."

Thursday, September 3 at 4:50 p.m.

When Jo and Pete walked into the Paradise Lounge, there were already several people sitting at the bar enjoying happy hour. Jo spotted Reece shaking a canister behind the bar. They stood at the corner of the bar and waited as Reece finished pouring the drink. Reece's smile disappeared when she spotted them. Jo walked closer. "Hello, Reece, I'm afraid I have some bad news for you. Can we talk?"

The young woman stopped what she was doing

behind the bar and strolled towards Jo and Pete. She crossed her arms.

Jo said, "I'm sorry to have to tell you this, but Sarah was found dead today in her home."

Reece stared as if she didn't quite comprehend Jo's words. She held her hands to her face and cried. "No, no, no. What? How can this happen?" Reece wiped her wet face. "Sarah was the best. She had such a good heart. I just told her the other day she was pretty and could do anything she wanted."

Jo stepped closer. "Reece, I'm so sorry. I know Sarah was your friend more so than Laura, but we really need your help. Why don't we walk over here so you don't upset your customers?"

Reece shuddered. Her tears spilled down her face making her seem young and vulnerable. "This is probably all Laura's fault. Right? She's still messing up people's lives even though she's dead."

Jo noticed Reece's boss look with concern in their direction. She did a head nod to Pete, directing his attention to the manager. Pete returned her head nod and walked over to the manager, while Jo pulled Reece to the side. "Reece, we need to know more about this guy you saw Laura with."

Reece whined. "What? Why? That was only one time."

"Are you sure he hasn't been in here again?"

Reece took a deep breath and wiped her face with a sleeve, smearing her mascara down her cheeks.

Jo looked around and grabbed napkins from a dispenser off a table. "Here."

Reece took the napkins. Jo waited as Reece tried to make her face more presentable. "Thanks. Why do you want to find this guy? Did he do this to Sarah?"

"We don't know yet, but we think Sarah may have had contact with him."

Reece took a deep sigh. "I'm serving drinks all the time. I know my regulars. I haven't seen that guy again, although he could have been here before. So you think he killed Sarah and Laura? Why Sarah?"

"I don't know, but he's the only lead we have now, Reece. Sarah thought she saw him recently, but that he looked different. He could be someone you've seen before, but maybe something about him looked different so you didn't really recognize him."

Reece shook her head. "Like a new haircut or maybe he changed his hair color?"

Jo thought for a minute. "Or contact lenses. Sarah mentioned the guy had really blue eyes. What do you remember about his eyes?"

"I was far away. I couldn't tell you his eye color. Just that he was tall, with black hair. His hair was short on the sides and full at top like he used mousse or something to make it stand up."

Jo pulled out her card. "Okay, Reece. I may have given you my card before, but I really need you to let me know if you remember anything else or if you see the guy again."

Jo turned to walk away, but Reece called out.

"Wait, I remember something when Sarah and I were talking not too long ago. I asked her how she felt about Laura cheating on Matt. Sarah was really angry. I remember she said one of these days Laura was going to get caught."

Jo inquired, "Was there something that prompted Sarah to say that?"

"I remember Sarah saying if she was going to cheat, not that she would, but she would at least go someplace where no one would see her having an affair."

Jo thought about Bryan. His affair happened out

of town at a conference in Atlanta. Her older half-brother, Jax, lived in Atlanta. Still, it was a big city.

Reece continued, "Sarah said Laura was seen at Ryder's. It's a restaurant not too far from where Matt worked. That's pretty risky."

Jo frowned. "Sarah never mentioned that to me. Did she say she saw Laura with a man?"

"No, Sarah didn't see them, but she had an ex-boyfriend that works at Ryder's. They're still friends...or they were. Anyway, he was the one who mentioned seeing Laura with some guy."

Jo wasn't sure if this lead would help or not, but knowing someone else saw her person of interest felt like an unopened Christmas gift to her. "Do you have his name? I need to talk to him."

Chapter 17

Monday, September 7 at 1:20 p.m.

Labor Day

It was Labor Day and normally for the long weekend, Jo spent time with her family. Today, she turned down her parents' invitation to attend the last barbecue of the season. Bryan took the opportunity to take B.J. out for some fun at Chuck E. Cheese. Normally, this would have been a family outing and B.J. seemed sad when she told him she couldn't go. She simply didn't have the energy to be around Bryan.

Jo curled up on the couch wrapped in her pink terry cloth robe alone with her thoughts on her first day off in a while. There was never really a time when she could turn her thoughts off from work. Nothing was happening with either Laura or Sarah's cases, which made her wandering mind even more frustrated. Every time they had a lead it fizzled or moved forward in slow motion.

She had not been able to make contact with Sarah's ex-boyfriend, Scott Russo. He was not only out-of-town, but out-of-the country in Italy for several weeks. Jo hoped to touch base with Scott soon, even if it was a long-distance call. She was desperate, but her hope waned that Scott would remember anything. After all, she was depending on Scott's memory and so far everyone else was not helping.

Sarah's death bothered Jo. Somehow, she felt responsible. She was sure Sarah went a little further than she should have and made contact with her killer. *Why didn't Sarah come to me?*

It also didn't help Jo to know that in a week she was expected to be ready to testify on the stand for the prosecution. Jo hadn't seen Jeffrey Maddock in ten months. While she didn't get a full confession from him, the hours she'd spent interrogating Maddock was enough to solidify that the hunt for a serial killer had ended. She couldn't help but think about the two recent deaths. They were so different and not very consistent.

The doorbell rang jarring Jo's thoughts. Jo

glanced at the wall clock in the living room. Bryan and B.J. had only been gone a little over an hour. She moved her legs out from under her and went towards the door.

"Who is it?"

"It's Asia."

Jo tilted her head. "Asia? Hold on." She rarely received a visit from her older sister. Not that they weren't close, but they both led very busy and separate lives. Jo opened the door to find her sister dressed fashionably even with a t-shirt and jeans. Jo glanced down to see her sister's feet, usually clad in three-inch heels in a bright blue pair of Sketchers.

"You look like you're enjoying your Labor Day."

Asia arched her right eyebrow and moved past Jo into the hallway. "What about you? You have everyone worried. You know Jax made it in from Atlanta. He's staying with our parents."

Jo shut the door. "I knew there was some reason you were standing at my door. When are you going to get along with Jax? If Mama can accept him as family, don't you think you should too? Nothing can change him being our half-brother."

Asia whipped her neck causing her ponytail to swing around her head. "I know that. I just don't like him. He may be blood, but he's also the most arrogant man I know."

Jo smirked. "Knowing how many lawyers you know and have dated, I would say that's an exaggeration. Jax isn't all that bad."

Asia followed Jo into the living room. Jo flopped back down on the couch while Asia stood.

"You can have a seat, Asia. My living room is not off limits like Mama's had her living room all our lives."

"Girl, I know. I didn't want to barge in on you." Asia cocked her ear to the door. I don't hear little B.J."

"He's out with his Bryan."

Asia backed up towards a chair. She sat and looked at Jo. "So, what's going on with you and Bryan? Is that why you're here in a funk instead of with your family? Mama's worried about you." Asia dug in her pocket. "Anyway, I've been meaning to give this to you." She reached over and handed Jo a card.

Somehow Jo knew what it was before she flipped the business card over in her hand.

Sandra Michaels. Divorce lawyer.

Jo flicked the card back towards her sister. "Is this your way of being helpful?"

Asia sighed and bent down to grab the card. "What is wrong with you, Jo? Sandra is the best if you need to have someone who can make sure you get custody of B.J."

"I don't want to think about that and for now nothing is going on. We're just co-existing."

"Well, that can't be good for anyone. Now, I'm worried about you. Everybody is worried. You seem more withdrawn."

"It's not all Bryan. He's part of it." Jo bit her lip. "These new cases too."

Asia sat back, "Well, I know you ending up with Senator Finney's daughter's case was not good for you. What about this other chick that was killed last week? I saw on the news that they knew each other."

Jo nodded. "They were friends."

Asia asked, "So, it wasn't the fiancé?"

Jo crossed her arms. "Matt. He was the ex-fiancé. He had motive for Laura, but no. Sarah, the other girl, was his cousin as well as his alibi. We're investigating some new leads now."

"Mmm, these cases do sound complicated, sis. I know you can handle them. I am concerned though. You do know Maddock's trial starts next week? We'll probably want to put you on the stand first. Are you going to be able to handle facing him?"

"Of course. Why wouldn't I? It's my job and Maddock is going down. I promised those women's families he wouldn't ever leave prison. I hope the jury is ready."

"Girl, the district attorney's office is not going to have any trouble convincing a jury. We're hoping his defense team will be bold enough to put Maddock on the stand. He will be ripped apart."

Jo laughed. "I doubt seriously Maddock's lawyers are going to let him open his mouth. He's so smug and the sad thing is, he can't help himself."

Asia shook her head. "You're right about that. I know you'll do fine, but I'm still worried about you."

"Why?"

"You're struggling, sis. I can tell. Everyone can tell. You love Bryan and you're hurt. If it was me, I would've kicked Bryan out and kept it moving."

"It's not that simple, Asia."

"I know, I know. Just don't sacrifice yourself in order to stay strong for B.J. You're more like mama. You will suffer, but then again I know you will pray too."

"Prayer is keeping me sane. This case is driving

me crazy and Bryan has indicated he doesn't like my obsessive behaviors."

"Girl, don't tell me he's trying to use that as some excuse for his affair?"

"He didn't voice it like that, but he's unhappy with how much time I spend on cases. I can't pretend like last year I didn't pull away from being a real mother to B.J."

"Oh come on. Jo, you're the best detective on the force. You're an awesome mom too. B.J. is proud of you and you are there for him. You're not like our dad. You remember growing up, how often we didn't see him, and all the things he missed."

Jo's eyes watered and she blinked. "I've missed out on things too, Asia."

Asia got up and sat on the couch. She grabbed Jo's hands. "It's not all of the time. You're conscience of your son's needs. I've seen you. All of us have. You've been there for Bryan too. I mean, do I need to *remind* you of a few things because you know I will."

Jo snatched her hands away from Asia. "Don't go there!"

"Oh yes, I will. Now that I know Bryan is putting pressure on you about your work. I mean thank God he finally got a real job and put that entrepreneurship phase to rest. Did he not realize how much stress he was putting you under? He should be supporting you like you supported him."

"We've both been guilty."

Asia pulled the business card out again. "If you need this, I can still leave it with you."

Jo looked at the card. "I'm angry with Bryan, but I'm not sure I want to go down that road yet."

Asia rolled her eyes. "Well, Mama said marriage counseling was supposed to be another option."

"I have thought about it, but I'm not sure I want to share my private life with someone, which in this case would probably be Pastor Freeman." She looked at her sister and held out her hand.

Asia placed the business card in Jo's hand. "You're a good mother and you've been a good wife. Bryan needs to appreciate all that you do and support you. All of your cases don't pull you away. It's only a few cases."

"Maybe a few cases too many for Bryan," Jo said.

"Mama, look what I got!"

She hadn't heard the front door open. She turned to see B.J. holding a large bag in his hand. He walked towards her. She looked behind B.J. Bryan stood in the doorway. He stared at her, then at Asia with questions in his eyes.

How long had he'd been standing there?

"Hey, Aunt Asia. I didn't know you were coming."

As Asia bent down to hug B.J., Jo looked back at Bryan and watched as he walked away from the living room. Asia was her most difficult sibling. She was not afraid to stir up drama. Bryan knew to stay away from her older sister.

Jo looked down at the card for a moment, and then slipped it into her robe pocket. She didn't know if she wanted to thank her sister or not, but something jolted inside of her. It was past time to stop stalling and make a decision.

September 7 at 10:37 p.m.

Before heading to bed, Jo did something she hadn't done in a while. She'd been praying, but she hadn't picked up her Bible, which rested on the nightstand under the iPad. Jo loved reading, especially the Bible, but she had not been on a regular reading plan since the case last year. Normally, she would reach for the Bible app on the iPad, but she wanted to feel the Bible in her hand. It was the same Bible her mother gave her when she'd been promoted to detective. At the time, Jo thought it was an unconventional gift. But then,

Jo had seen the worst sides of people and often needed to be reminded that God was sovereign.

After she opened the Bible, she reached for her iPad, pulling up the Bible app since it was great for quick searches. She searched for the word divorce and read through several passages. The verse that seemed to strike her attention was in the book of Matthew, chapter nineteen, verse three. She especially focused on the passages written in red to signify that Jesus was talking. In this passage, the Pharisees tried to trick Jesus by asking him, "Is it lawful for a man to divorce his wife for any and every reason?"

Jo thought to herself, "What about a woman?" Knowing during the Bible times, women were not seen the same as today, she pressed on to read Jesus' words. "*...at the beginning the Creator made them male and female,' and said, 'For this reason a man will leave his father and mother and be united to his wife and the two will become one flesh. So they are not longer two, but one flesh. Therefore what God has joined together, let no one separate.'*

Jo focused on the passage that said, let no one separate. She thought about her vows almost seven years ago. She thought about life before she'd met Bryan and then their first date. Asia had reminded her of all the financial ups and downs during the first years of their marriage and all of Bryan's attempts to keep his online business going. Jo's frustrations had often lingered. There were times when she wanted to give up on him, but she hadn't.

The business card Asia gave her earlier seemed to being calling to Jo from her robe, which lay across the bed. She reached over to grab the robe, feeling for the card in the pocket. She pulled it out and looked at the attorney's name. If she called, what would happen? What would this person say to her?

Jo still didn't feel like this was what she wanted. She tucked the card in her Bible as a bookmark for the verses in the book of Matthew. She placed the book and iPad back on her nightstand and knelt beside the bed.

God, Bryan and I can't stay like this. I know I don't feel right about breaking up our family even though I'm still hurt by Bryan's betrayal. I don't know if I can trust him again. He's a good father and I feel like we still love each other, but we're stuck. Will you give us both the wisdom we need to make the best decision for all of us? I see enough pain every day and I've been in pain. I want to be able to move forward.

In Jesus' name. Amen.

Chapter 18

Tuesday, September 8 at 11:03 a.m.

Thanks to a restful night's sleep, Jo sat at her desk fully engaged for a change. Earlier this morning she'd finally talked to Scott Russo, Sarah's ex-boyfriend. Someone in his family told him what happened to Sarah and the poor guy hopped on a plane back to the United States over the weekend. Jo was thankful, because Scott had encountered the man he saw with Laura on more than one occasion.

Jo asked him, "Would you say he was a regular at the restaurant?"

Scott answered, "I wouldn't say I've seen him every day or every week, but he has eaten at the restaurant a few times. When he does come in, it's usually during the lunch hour and he orders the same thing. He may have been on some diet, because he always ordered the double Angus burger without the bread, medium rare with a side salad. Just water to drink. One time I asked him if he wanted to try the special for the day, he almost looked offended. He said he didn't like change. He liked what he likes."

"Do you recall if he paid with a credit card?"

Jo cringed as Scott stated, "Sorry, he was a cash only guy. He left great tips."

Despite jet lag, Scott was willing to share what he remembered with a sketch artist. Jo looked at the time. She'd requested for her sister Toni to come in and work with Scott on a sketch.

While she waited, she decided to review Maddock's case files since she would be called in about a week to take the stand at trial. In the back of her mind, she hoped nothing would pop up to make her doubt their work on that case. She also thought it was a good idea to check for any missing loose ends. So far there were no clear connections to Maddock and Laura or Sarah's cases, which would have been pretty impossible since the guy had been in prison.

Still, there was the copycat theory that both her and Pete bounced around with hesitancy. Jo couldn't shake the similar patterns, especially in the victim's appearance and the manner in which they were killed. Sarah in particular. She made a note to get a record of Maddock's correspondence from prison as well as any visitors. She hated to follow up Pete's craziest theory, but Jo wanted to be assured Maddock wasn't influencing someone outside of prison.

She scoured the interview notes, searching for anyone in Maddock's circle who may have been extra loyal or a devout fan. Most people thought Maddock was a charming, handsome man with no family. His friends were shocked by his arrest, and those a bit closer commented they'd always wondered why the forty-five year old never married. While he was friendly enough, he was a bit standoffish. What Jo saw was an intelligent, manipulative man who patiently waited to do his evil deeds.

Maddock never showed anger as they accused him of his crimes. Even more disturbing, he neither denied nor confirmed his involvement. What remained the same was the persistent smirk that lifted the right side of his face in an odd way, marring his good looks. Jo was not looking forward to facing him again in a courtroom, but she had to make sure he and his arrogance stayed behind bars for a long time, preferably for life.

She leaned back in her chair to rest her eyes. Her eyes landed on a photo of Sarah. Sarah's death was unexpected. Jo still reeled with shock. She was sure Sarah's assailant attacked her in a fit of rage. Jo wondered if Sarah had found out anything before she could share it with them.

There was no turning back now, but Jo really wished they had not spent so much time focused on Matt because finding this other guy in Laura's life had become maddening to Jo. Witnesses were notorious for getting details wrong. However, in this case no one could give her much more than a generic description of the man. It was like he purposely made sure he stayed hidden in the shadows so no one would recognize him later.

We are going to find you soon!

Jo stood and stretched her arms above her head. From behind her, she heard, "Jo, here is what I have."

Jo turned around to see her younger sister standing with a folder in her hand. She had to grin. The free spirit of the family surprised them all when she finally settled down to use her artistic talent in a forensic career. It was still hard to believe. "I hope Scott gave you something to work with for the sketch."

"He did his best. He was really upset about losing his girlfriend. He kept correcting himself saying she was really his ex-girlfriend. I could tell the poor guy was still in love with her." Toni held out the folder. "At least now you have a face for your mystery suspect."

Jo took the folder from Toni, but hesitated for a moment like she had to prepare herself for what she was about see. She flipped the folder open and stared at the sketch. Jo frowned.

Why did this guy seem so familiar to her?

"What are you thinking, Jo?"

Jo focused on Toni, who peered at her over her thick-framed glasses. "You did a great job. I just can't shake this feeling that I've seen this guy before."

"Well, I know you'll find him, Jo. If anyone can, you can, sis."

Jo hugged her sister. As she watched Toni walk away, she noticed Pete coming towards her with the captain not far behind him.

Upon approach, Pete asked, "Do we have a face?"

Jo handed over the sketch and watched as Pete examined the sketch and then the captain.

Pete voiced out loud, "Is it just me or does this guy look like he could be Maddock's brother?"

A slow tense pounding formed around her temples. *Is that what's bothering me?* She didn't recall Maddock having any siblings. "I've been looking at Maddock's case files all morning. He had no family. It was him and his mom. She's been dead ten years. I do think we need to look a little more closely at who's visited or corresponded with Maddock."

Pete raised an eyebrow. "So my crazy theory about Maddock being involved is sounding plausible now?"

Captain nodded in agreement. "I agree it may not be a bad idea. You both need to cover any ground you can so we can keep the D.A. up to speed on anything that could throw the Maddock trial off course."

Pete asked, "So what do we do with the composite? Do we want to send this to the media now?"

The captain pondered Pete's question for a few seconds before responding. "Show it around discreetly for now. Start with the places this guy has been seen already. Somebody has to know this guy personally and can give us a name."

Jo was thinking the same thing. They were closer than they had been in weeks.

Chapter 19

Wednesday, September 9 at 9:18 a.m.

Jo was not looking forward to paying the Finneys a visit, but they needed Laura's parents to know they had a possible suspect. Jo regretted being assigned to this task while Pete went to show the sketch around at Ryder's restaurant. They agreed that to cover as much ground as possible, they needed to split up.

Senator Finney examined the sketch and then passed it to his wife. He stated, "I've never seen him before. Was he someone who went to Duke with Laura?"

Jo had tossed the idea around to Pete earlier since they had not reached out to any of Laura's Duke classmates. All the sightings of the man with Laura had been during the summer while she was home. They both agreed this man had to live here in Charlotte.

Dressed in the same robe as the first time Jo came to the house, Mrs. Finney examined the sketch for a full minute. She practically shoved the sketch back at Jo. "I don't think I know him either. Who is he?"

Jo observed Mrs. Finney's face. Something about the sketch had disturbed her, but she was putting on a good face for her husband. "We're still tracking down leads to find this person. Are you sure you've never seen him before?"

Senator Finney frowned. "We just said we've never seen the man before. I don't understand why you're showing him to us. Is he a suspect? How would Laura know him?"

Jo caught Mrs. Finney's eyes. They were the eyes of a woman in pain, but she also saw something else. The woman stared back at her as though to warn her not to say a word. Laura was probably a daddy's girl and Mrs. Finney had become accustomed to protecting Laura's image.

Senator Finney continued his tirade, "Are you posting this where others can report sightings of this man? Shouldn't you be setting up a manhunt?"

"Whoa, sir! We don't want to waste the

department resources dragging any old poor soul in for questioning. We also don't want to risk our possible suspect fleeing the area. We're gathering evidence so we can make an arrest."

Senator Finney crossed his arms. "I hope you know what you're doing. Is it Detective Reed, you say? You seem to have wasted quite a bit of time with Matt. Matt's family didn't deserve to be pulled through the mud by the media."

"That was unfortunate. The media took that to another level by themselves. Look, we will find this man. I'll keep you updated."

Jo turned to leave the room. The senator was a grieving father, but she'd had enough of being in his presence.

Mrs. Finney followed behind her. "Let me walk you out, Detective."

"I think I can find my way out, Mrs. Finney."

"I insist. Besides, I need some fresh air."

Jo looked at the woman and then nodded. She sensed Mrs. Finney had something else on her mind. Most mothers knew more about their children's habits than they often let on. After they stepped outside, Mrs. Finney clawed at her throat as though she had something choking her that she wanted to get out.

Jo nudged gently, "Are you okay?"

Mrs. Finney clasped her hands together. She didn't look directly at Jo, but off in the distance towards a garden on the left. "Laura and I argued before she left that night. I brought her some new wedding magazines and she snapped at me. It was like she suddenly didn't want to talk about the wedding anymore. I thought maybe her and Matt had an argument."

The woman looked at Jo. "When you questioned Matt, I was hoping he hadn't hurt my Laura. I believed he loved her. Then poor Sarah." Mrs. Finney placed her hands on the sides of her face. "Sarah was so loyal to Laura. I just don't understand why this has all happened."

Jo wanted the woman to focus. "Mrs. Finney, the man in the sketch, did the face remind you of someone? Maybe you saw Laura with him?"

Mrs. Finney looked directly at Jo. "I do feel like I've seen that face before. I could be wrong, but I think the man you showed me was Matt's friend."

Jo's heart pounded in her chest. "Wait, you think you saw this guy with Matt?"

"Matt proposed here at our home last Christmas. We insisted Laura and Matt celebrate their engagement on New Year's. They both invited friends. I don't remember this man's name, but I remember he stood in a corner most of the time."

Jo added, "Like he felt out of place?"

Mrs. Finney nodded. "Yes. I thought it was also odd and it could've just been me, but he couldn't take his eyes off Laura. I remembering thinking to myself, where did Matt find such a strange friend? I'm sorry, I don't know why I never thought about this before."

"Thank you, Mrs. Finney. That's really very helpful. I will stay in touch with you."

Jo climbed into her car and watched as Mrs. Finney went back inside. Her eyes moved up the side of the house where something twinkled in the sunlight. She leaned further towards the passenger side of the car so she could see. There was a camera pointing towards the driveway. She scolded herself for not noticing it before. They needed to get access to that camera's footage.

She drove like a madwoman from the Finneys' house back to the station. On her way back to her desk, Sgt. Wu met her in the hallway. "Hey, Detective Reed. I have something you might want to see."

"Good. I may need your help with something else on the Finney case."

Jo followed Wu to the room where other techs were working on various computers. A lot of cybercrime activities were monitored in this area. Jo recognized Laura's laptop on Wu's desk.

Wu pulled out a chair for Jo to sit. "This took longer than expected because some of Laura's accounts were not accessible. We finally got into her Facebook account and I think I found some interesting correspondence."

"Really? So she communicated with this guy via Facebook?"

"Yes, in fact the Facebook Messenger app seemed to be the main way she communicated with him. There were no emails and I couldn't find any text messages. From what I can tell Laura started communicating in early June with this guy."

Jo observed the profile Wu pulled up. The dark haired man had vivid blue eyes. "Daniel Lewis? Well, he matches the sketch and previous descriptions." As Jo stared at the photo she had that strange feeling again that she'd seen this man before. He did remind her of Maddock. Now why was that?

Wu continued, "The last message between this

guy and Laura coincides with the night Laura died. It appears she was going out to dinner with him."

"Did they mention a restaurant?"

Wu shook his head, "Nope. The guy is either a romantic or he wanted to keep the details a secret. Also, he does not have many friends and he rarely posts. It's like he just logs in to chat with Laura. Anyway, we're running his name through our databases to see if we can get any matches. We're assuming Daniel Lewis is his real name, but you never know."

Jo mentioned, "Wu, I know how we might be able to get some more info on this guy. The first time I talked to Mrs. Finney she said someone picked Laura up from the house that night. At the time, I assumed it was one of the friends, but they didn't go out together. The Finneys have at least one camera on the property pointed towards the driveway. Can we get access to that camera from the security company, in particular, for any activity on August 18th? Maybe we can get this guy's license plate."

Based on her talk with Mrs. Finney, it was time to pay Matt Vaynor a visit again. They needed to know which one of Matt's friends were not what they appeared to be.

Chapter 20

Thursday, September 10 at 3:07 p.m.

Pete shook his head as he drove. "Why didn't I think about the Finneys having a camera? They have the money for a serious security system. So what do we know about our guy now?"

Jo replied, "Wu said he was able to get the footage and it clearly showed a black car coming by to pick up Laura. The driver never got out, but Wu said they're trying to blow up the image to get the license plate."

Pete tapped the steering wheel. "Didn't Sarah mention to you about seeing a guy get out a black car near Matt's apartment?"

"She did and Mrs. Finney thinks our guy was a friend of Matt's. Some friend!"

Pete sighed. "Why do we always have the

unfortunate job of investigating the craziest of the crazy people in Charlotte?"

Jo shrugged. "It does feel like that sometimes. I hope Matt is up to seeing us. The receptionist told me earlier he hasn't been to work since Sarah's death. Poor guy is going to lose his job."

After Pete found a parking space outside of Matt's building, they moved quickly up the stairs to his apartment. Pete banged on the door two times before Matt opened the door.

From the looks of Matt's disheveled clothes, he hadn't been very functional in days. Jo concluded that he'd been drinking.

Matt grimaced when he saw them. "Go away!" He tried closing the door, but Pete pushed the door, sending Matt scrambling backwards.

"Mr. Vaynor, if you really want to do something for Laura and Sarah, you will help us out here."

Jo stepped inside the apartment and watched the turmoil on Matt's face. This guy needed help before he self-destructed.

Pete asked, "Do you know a Daniel Lewis?"

Matt shouted and began pacing. "Who? No! Why can't you just leave me alone?"

Jo tried to calm him down. "Matt, please. We need information and you're the only one who can help us. Mrs. Finney said you brought a guy with you to the New Year's Eve party when you celebrated your engagement to Laura. Who was that guy, Matt?"

Matt fell back on his couch. He appeared confused. "Josh?"

She glanced at Pete, who looked equally confused. She asked, "Josh? Your co-worker?"

Matt shrugged. "He had nothing to do on New Year's Eve. He's a cool guy, not many friends. I felt sorry for him and told him to come celebrate. I'm pretty sure he regretted coming because he left without saying goodbye. At work, he seemed offended I'd invited him."

"How so?"

"He wouldn't talk to me for a while. I couldn't figure out what I did wrong. He eventually came around."

Jo processed what Matt was saying. "So Laura met Josh at this party?"

Matt snorted. "I think I introduced them. I doubt she would have remembered him. Laura was in her own world that night."

Jo tried to make the connections in her head, but she was still confused. "So you said you and Josh weren't talking for a while and then everything was good. Did Josh help you move out of your house last month?"

Matt nodded. "Yes, he offered to help me move. He showed up first. We actually packed a lot on the truck before my other friends arrived."

Jo remembered Matt mentioning the rug was supposedly placed on the truck first. She wondered if Josh had a hand in making sure the rug went missing.

"Laura was there helping out too?"

Matt looked at Jo. "Why are you asking all of these questions?"

"We're trying to establish some things. Now tell me, did Laura help you move?"

"She came by later, her and Sarah. Now that you ask, I remember Josh left. I don't know. He didn't seem very comfortable around women."

Pete commented, "Really? So you don't think he had a girlfriend?"

Matt eyed them wearily. "I don't know. We worked together, but we're not that close. He did seem happier about something or someone this summer. Look, I'm not feeling so good. Are we finished?"

Pete stated, "Not yet."

Jo noticed Matt's face had become even paler.

"Let me ask you one more question. What kind of car does Josh drive?"

Matt squinted as if he was trying to focus his thoughts. "A Honda, I think. It's black and an older model. Maybe 2005 or something like that. Look, I don't know why you have these questions about Josh, but I think... I'm going to be sick."

Matt jumped up from the couch and ran towards the back of the apartment. A few minutes later, Jo cringed as she heard Matt letting out his insides.

Jo and Pete quietly let themselves out of Matt's apartment.

Pete ran his hand through his hair as they walked back to the car. "So is Josh Collins the same person as Daniel Lewis?"

"I really don't know. I remember seeing the guy that one time when we went to Matt's office. He was wearing glasses, so it's possible. Mrs. Finney did say the guy at the party couldn't take his eyes off Laura. Maybe Josh decided to pursue Laura for whatever reason."

Pete clicked the car doors open with his key fob. "Sounds like something set him off. He wasn't too happy with Matt for a while. I'm wondering if he went after Laura to get back at Matt."

After they entered the car, Jo said, "You know

both Matt and Laura came from pretty influential, wealthy homes. The party at the Finneys could have messed with the guy's head too. I don't know. I just know two young women have been senselessly killed."

Jo's phone rang. She looked at the screen. "Wait, don't start the car yet. This is Wu. He may have more from that camera footage." She answered the phone. "Wu, what do you have for us?"

"Well, we were able to get the plates off the Honda and run them. But you may not like what I have to tell you next."

Jo frowned. "What do you mean?"

"The name and the photo that shows up with this car registration does not look anything like Daniel Lewis from the Facebook profile."

"What? Text the photo to me."

Jo waited for the message to arrive and clicked on the picture. She gasped and turned her phone so Pete could see the driver's license. "The car used to pick up Laura that night is registered to a Josh Collins. But this is the real Josh Collins."

Pete swore. "Get out of here! That guy is at least twenty years older and bald. Who's the guy that works with Matt? Who are we looking for then?"

"That's a good question." Jo realized they were

dealing with someone even scarier than she thought. Someone who'd stolen an identity. *Where was the real Josh Collins? Had he been murdered too?*

Chapter 21

Friday, September 11 at 10:07 p.m.

The night air was cool. The thick clouds threatened rain. Jo's backside had grown tired from sitting in the car with Pete for two hours. There were still no signs of their suspect, who they referred to as Daniel Lewis. It took them some time working with Ridgecrest Construction's human resources department, but they'd finally located and scoped out the two-story brick home where Daniel lived under the alias Josh Collins.

The real Josh Collins had died five years ago supposedly from a drug overdose. How Daniel acquired the identity was not really clear yet. All they knew was he'd been in the Charlotte area working at Ridgecrest Construction for a year using the name Josh Collins. According to Laura's phone records, the house fit into the same area where Laura's phone was last pinged. The crime scene could have been inside.

Jo wasn't happy they had to do a stakeout, but their best bet was to lay in wait to see if the man pretending to be Josh Collins returned to his home. Her search for the name Daniel Lewis between the ages of 25 and 35 brought up a large number of results. There was still no telling their suspect's real identity without DNA. During their briefing, Daniel was to be considered dangerous, since he reportedly killed two women that they knew of, and had adopted a deceased man's identity. The captain worked it out with Judge James Thompson to issue a "no knock" search warrant. It was a risky approach, and Jo wasn't sure she was comfortable with the plan.

Something could go wrong.

This was the first time in a long time she'd been on a stakeout. She'd gone home long enough to change into jeans and grab a bite to eat. The look on B.J.'s face when she had to explain to him, once again, that she would not see him at bedtime crushed her. Bryan's face was blank and lacked emotion. Jo could no longer deny she was starting to despise the work she loved especially with her crumbling marriage hanging in the balance.

Both she and Pete periodically checked in with backup, which was discreetly standing by. She turned to Pete who had nodded off despite guzzling down a cup of coffee forty-five minutes ago. She snapped her fingers and then snickered as Pete's eyes flipped wide open. "I hope he's coming back tonight, 'cause you look like you're not going to make it."

Pete slumped down in the seat more. "I'm getting too old for this, kid. I hope this guy, whatever his name, hasn't already hauled it out of dodge or none of us will be sleeping any time soon. He hasn't shown up to work for two days now, claiming to be sick. And, he's not been here. This guy could be getting ready to change identities again. For all we know, he may have some other crimes we're not aware of. "

Jo agreed. "I know. I touched base with Matt. He told me he hasn't talked to Josh. I don't know what this guy has been up to, but he's coming back. There's no reason for him to be spooked unless his crimes have him extra anxious. Still, he wouldn't have just left this place like it was without removing any traces of himself."

Pete crossed his arms over his chest. "True. If he doesn't eventually come back, we need to get inside to get his DNA and see if we can pull it up in the system."

In the right side mirror, Jo noticed approaching lights entering the subdivision. She slid down, "Well, someone is arriving home rather late now."

Pete's eyes were wide as he observed through the rear view mirror. "It does look like that black Honda. We might be in luck."

More like an answer to prayer. Jo didn't agree on the luck part. She'd been praying for them to get this guy since she left her home earlier. It was time to close these cases.

They waited for the car to pull into the driveway and watched as a man stepped out of the driver's side.

Jo strained her eyes in the dark, hoping the lamp post by the house next door would shine some light on the man's face. *It was him!* He was the same man they saw in Matt's office the first time. The man looked around as though he could feel them watching him. He pushed his glasses up on his nose. She kept him under surveillance as he moved briskly towards the house.

They waited a full three minutes after he went

inside the house before Pete called in on the walkie-talkie. "We got eyes on our suspect. Let's move."

Jo slipped out the car and followed behind Pete. Her bulletproof vest felt heavy and stiff against her chest. They didn't know who they were dealing with so all precautions were necessary. From her right side, she spotted members of her team making their way around the house. If there were any lights on in the house, none were visible from the street.

Sgt. Vince Knight came up beside them. "We'll go in first and announce we have a search warrant and bring this guy out."

Jo nodded and pulled her Glock from her holster. "Let's do this."

They slowly approached the door. Jo held her gun out in front of her and then glanced at Pete, who looked significantly more alert than he did fifteen minutes ago.

She heard Knight shout, "Police! Search warrant." In only a few seconds, the front door was crashed in and they were inside.

Up ahead, Jo heard Knight repeat, "We have a search warrant. Please come out with your hands up." Knight said over his shoulders, "Locate the suspect."

The house was dark. *Where is this guy?* She didn't have a good feeling about this. She pulled her flashlight out of her holster, holding it above her shoulder.

Above their heads on the second floor, Jo heard sounds of feet running and then a door slam. She flicked her flashlight towards the stairs.

"Let's go. That has to be him upstairs." It was time to stop playing. She wanted to catch this guy.

Jo climbed the stairs, gun and flashlight out in front of her with Pete close behind. When she reached the top of the stairs, she noticed movement to her right and swung the flashlight in that direction. She didn't see anyone in the hall. All the doors on the second floor were closed.

Pete said behind her, "He's hiding. I'm calling for backup to get up here." He held is walkie-talkie. "Requesting backup. We have activity upstairs."

Jo continued down the hallway towards the door where she sensed movement. She grabbed the handle of the door and pushed it open. She quickly pulled the gun and flashlight in front of her. The light bounced around in what appeared to be a bedroom. As Jo swung the flashlight around, she gasped. She realized something or someone was coming towards her.

"Stop or I will shoot. Come out with your hands up where I can see them."

Out of the darkness, Daniel's face appeared in front of her. He stared back at her. His eyes displayed no emotions.

Jo held his gaze. She cocked her gun towards him. "Don't make this hard. Come out nice and slow."

His mouth broke into a smile. "I can't do that."

She hoped Pete and the rest of the team were not far behind. It suddenly felt like it was just her and this guy. Jo grasped her gun tighter, her finger on the trigger.

"Don't do anything stupid. Just come out with your hands up."

Daniel said, "I control my fate."

Before Jo fully comprehended what he meant, his hand raised towards his head.

"No!" Jo shouted.

The gunshot rang in her ears. She could hear shouts behind her.

With the gunshot still ringing in her ears, Jo reached inside the room and felt for a light switch on the wall. Daniel's body slid down the wall, smearing blood behind him. She didn't want to do it, but she walked over and placed her fingers on the side of his neck. As she stared down at him, he still had that same crazy smile on his face. Like somehow he'd won.

They were supposed to take him into custody and question him. She stepped back, realizing her body was shaking from the burst of adrenaline. She tore her eyes from the dead man to find Pete and Knight in the doorway.

Pete asked, "What happened? Did you shoot him?"

Jo shook her head. She was still trying to figure out exactly what happened. "He had a gun, but he aimed it at himself. He said, 'I control my fate.' I guess this was his way."

Pete swore. "It's like he knew we were coming. He made sure we couldn't bring him in."

Knight commented, "Like a rat backed up in a corner. I guess that was his way out. Looks like he had plenty to be guilty about."

Jo placed her gun back in her holster. She peered over at Daniel again. That was the first time in her career she'd ever had that happen. He just shot himself right in front of her. She didn't even realize he had a gun. He could have easily turned it on her.

Pete said behind her, "Let's get a CSI here."

Jo studied Daniel for another minute. She looked at his feet. "Tell CSI to bag his sneakers and check the closet for other sneakers. Let's see what else we can find."

They walked around the house, which now had every room lit up. It looked like any normal home that belonged to a bachelor. Jo went to the kitchen and decided to peek inside the fridge. The shelves were pretty bare. Either this guy ate out a lot or he was cleaning up, preparing to leave. She slammed the refrigerator door shut, frustrated that the man had taken his own life.

"Hey, Jo. Come take a look." Pete had stepped inside the kitchen.

Jo followed Pete down the hall into a small office. Pete pointed to the wall. "He'd been stalking Laura for some time." There were several photos of Laura pinned to the wall. Many of the photos were from Laura's beauty pageant days, with some being when she competed as a much younger pre-teen.

Jo thought for a minute. "So this guy knew Laura a lot longer than we were thinking. Remember our interviews with Micah and Reece? We know Laura was abrasive, could have been considered a mean girl. I wonder if there was something that happened a long time ago that set all of this in motion and this guy saw this as an opportunity to get to her."

Jo went behind the desk and pulled out the drawers. She pulled out papers, most of them with Josh Collins as the recipient. She pulled open a small drawer on the side of the desk. A photo sat very visible on top of the other items in the desk drawer. For a minute, she didn't know how to react to what she saw.

Pete asked, "Kid, you all right? What did you find over there?"

Jo looked back at Pete. "You may have been right."

Pete frowned, "About what?"

Jo gingerly pulled the photo from the drawer and placed it on the desk.

Pete shook his head. "What's this?"

Jo looked up at him. "This looks like our guy when he was a little boy. I'd say he was about six or seven, B.J.'s age in this photo."

He was a pudgy little boy wearing glasses even at that young age. Jo thought he was the kind of kid who was a target for a bully. "But that's not the most interesting part of this photo. Can't you see? Look closer." She pushed the photo towards Pete.

Pete bent down to examine the photo. "Maddock?"

Jo said, "Maddock never married, so we never looked for anything about him having a child. I'm going to revisit Maddock's visitors list tomorrow. There has always been something about Laura and then Sarah's deaths that seemed a little coincidental to me."

Chapter 22

Four weeks later

Monday, October 5 at 9:32 a.m.

Jo glanced down at the clock on her computer. She had less than thirty minutes before she had her meeting with the captain. She looked over her notes one last time, so she could officially close these cases in her mind. Though, she wasn't sure she really could. For several weeks, Jo couldn't let go of investigating Maddock's son.

She learned his real name was Daniel Collins. The man whose alias he'd adopted was, in fact, his uncle. Daniel's mother, Elizabeth Collins, was a heroin addict, who died while Daniel was in high school. The young man had dropped out of high school without anyone really keeping up with him. At some point along his journey, Jo concluded that

Daniel found out where his father presently lived and reconnected with him. It was Maddock's arrest that drew his son back to the Charlotte area.

She'd testified at Maddock's trial three weeks ago, and he was finally sentenced for life last week. During her testimony, Jo couldn't help but think as she observed Maddock that he was grinning at her. According to the prison visitation records, a man named Josh Collins had visited Maddock approximately three times in the last six months. The last time Daniel visited his father was a week prior to Laura's death.

Jo would never truly know what father and son talked about, but she felt like Daniel had somehow escaped justice. She had to come to terms that she did the best she could and God was the final judge. Jo also had to choose to take the road that would lead her back to her sanity and her life again. The clarity of what she needed to do was as clear as the yellow brick road in the Wizard of Oz. She'd never imagined she would do this, but it was the only thing that made sense to her.

When she talked to Bryan about what she was going to do, he looked at her as if he wanted to cry. He asked, "Are you sure you want to do this, Jo? That's pretty major."

She assured him she was at peace with her decision.

Jo looked at the clock again. *It's time.* She got up from her chair and walked towards the captain's office. When she entered, the captain and Pete both looked at her. She'd given a letter to the captain yesterday and told him she needed him to break the news to Pete first.

She sat in one of the other chairs across from the captain's desk. Finally Pete said, "Well, you got to do what you need to do, kid. I know this last case was rough."

Jo swallowed. "Sorry, Pete. I didn't know how to tell you." She looked at the captain. "Are we good?"

Captain Ransom answered back gruffly, "This is a difficult job, Detective. But, I understand your need to take some time off after these last couple of cases. I accept your leave of absence."

She placed her gun and badge on the captain's desk. Jo reached her hand out. The captain stood to shake her hand. "Thanks to the both of you."

Jo walked out with Pete trailing behind her. "I hope Bryan knows what kind of woman he has as his wife. Now you got me wanting to retire. What am I going to do without you, kid?"

She reached up and gave her partner a hug. "You'll survive. But, do me a favor. Find a way to get to know your kids again. Be happy, Pete. Get some joy in your life."

Pete smiled. "I hear you, kid. That's exactly what I'm going to do. I'll be in touch."

Jo snickered, knowing she would hear from Pete. She went inside her office and looked around. She could take unpaid leave up to twelve months if needed. Bryan promised her he could take care of the bills. That was good to know. Still in many ways she was going to miss the work, but she knew in time she'd be back.

God had promised her. She trusted Him.

Epilogue

Seven months later

May

Jo sat at the kitchen counter enjoying a cup of coffee. The warmth felt good flowing down her insides. Pete had been calling every other week to check on her, threatening to retire if she didn't come back soon. His new partner was a young guy whom Pete was apparently not getting along with. Unfortunately, Jo wasn't ready to go back yet. The timing still was not right.

At first, she didn't know what to do with all her free time. Then she began volunteering at B.J.'s school and then at Victory Gospel's women's shelter.

She had climbed out of the bed earlier, knowing in an hour she would wake up B.J. for school. He had a few more weeks before summer vacation started. For the summer, she already had activities planned for B.J. to keep learning. It was going to be an exciting couple of months.

We needed these changes. Thank you, Lord!

For a solid three months, Bryan had slept in the guest bedroom. Even after Bryan and she attended eight weeks of marriage counseling last fall, Jo still struggled. It wasn't until one night she woke deeply disturbed by a dream to find Bryan beside her. He'd prayed with her and then climbed beside her in bed. The next morning he asked her about the dream. She spilled it out to him as she would have in the past.

During their marriage counseling sessions, Reverend Freeman reminded them they were best friends and communication was key. It was a strange miracle, but Jo's nightmare about Maddock and his son broke down her walls for Bryan's return to the bedroom and to open a new chapter for their marriage.

Jo turned to see Bryan enter the kitchen. She smiled as she watched him grab a mug from the cabinet and pour coffee. The first few times had been awkward around her family, but everyone knew they were back together as a couple. While they didn't think B.J. had noticed, Jo's mother mentioned to her that because she and Bryan were happier, B.J. was happier.

Bryan sipped from his coffee. "Are you ready for me to wake up B.J.?"

Jo sighed and rubbed her stomach. "We can let him sleep a little longer. Remember, he doesn't have to get up as early since I'm dropping him off at school."

Bryan observed her. "You seem in a really good mood this morning. I assume you're feeling better."

Jo rinsed her mug out and placed it in the dishwasher. She'd been under the weather the past few days. She walked over to Bryan. "Well, the doctor said I definitely don't have the flu."

Bryan raised his eyebrow. "No? You were really ill. I could tell."

She nodded. "It was my body adjusting to a new addition."

"New addition?"

"We'll be doing a lot more Christmas shopping this year. Shopping for two, in fact."

Bryan's eyes grew wide. "You're pregnant?"

Jo nodded. "Yes."

Bryan wrapped his arms around Jo and picked her up off the floor. "Yes! Yes!"

As Bryan gently placed her feet back on the floor, he continued to hold her. Jo laid her head on his shoulder. She was thankful God had blessed them with another child, and even more thankful God had healed her broken heart.

Books by Tyora Moody

REED FAMILY SERIES
Broken Heart, Book 1

EUGEENA PATTERSON MYSTERIES
Oven Baked Secrets, Book 2
Deep Fried Trouble, Book 1
Shattered Dreams: A Short Story

SERENA MANCHESTER SERIES
Hostile Eyewitness, Book 1

VICTORY GOSPEL SERIES
When Perfection Fails, Book 3
When Memories Fade, Book 2
When Rain Falls, Book 1

About the Author

Tyora Moody is the author Soul-Searching Suspense novels in the Reed Family Series, Eugeena Patterson Mysteries, Serena Manchester Series, and the Victory Gospel Series. She is also the author of the nonfiction book, *The Literary Entrepreneur's Toolkit*, and the compilation editor for the Stepping Into Victory Compilations under her company, Tymm Publishing LLC.

To contact Tyora about book club discussions or for book marketing workshops, visit her online at TyoraMoody.com.